"Without the therapy I would never have decided to go in for reconstructive surgery. I think the doctor did a wonderful job. What do you think?"

In front of his disbelieving eyes, she removed the covers to reveal the length of her gorgeous body to his gaze. "Dr. Canfield told me only my husband would know for sure."

Her humor awed him.

Her courage moved him to tears.

The perfection of her figure left him without breath.

"Dominique—"

"I do believe my husband is speechless. I wonder if that's good or bad." She flashed him an impish smile, producing the dimple in her left cheek he hadn't seen for a year.

"Come to bed." She raised her soft, graceful arms toward him. "I've been waiting for this a long, long time."

Just like having a heart to heart with your best friend,
these stories will take you from laughter to tears
and back again!

Curl up and have a

Heart *to* Heart

with Harlequin Romance®

So heartwarming and emotional
you'll want to have some tissues handy!

Look out for more stories

in **HEART TO HEART**

coming soon to

Harlequin Romance®

HUSBAND BY REQUEST

Rebecca Winters

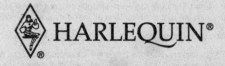

Heart *to* Heart

HARLEQUIN®

TORONTO • NEW YORK • LONDON
AMSTERDAM • PARIS • SYDNEY • HAMBURG
STOCKHOLM • ATHENS • TOKYO • MILAN • MADRID
PRAGUE • WARSAW • BUDAPEST • AUCKLAND

ISBN 0-373-03852-6

HUSBAND BY REQUEST

First North American Publication 2005.

CHAPTER ONE

"MOM? How do I look in this?" Dominique emerged from the bathroom of their hotel room in New York wearing a new yellow bikini.

Her mother gazed at her with loving, tear-filled eyes. "Absolutely beautiful."

"You know what I mean."

"The implant reconstruction is perfect. No one would ever know you had a breast removed."

"Andreas will notice the difference."

"Only in the privacy of your bedroom."

Dominique stared at her mother. "You mean only if he lets me get that close to him again."

"He will, because you'll find a way."

"Now that I've seen the doctor, there's no time to lose."

"You've stayed away from Andreas far too long as it is. Just remember that you were desirable to your husband before the reconstructive surgery. He married you after you had your mastectomy, and since you left him has patently refused to grant you a divorce. I don't see a problem."

Dominique saw a huge one. "It's been a horribly desolate year away from him, Mom. After the way I left him, he's not going to welcome me back with open arms."

"No. I'm sure he won't. But what he doesn't know is that you've been working hard at your marriage behind the scenes. Once he understands all you've gone through, and why, he'll love you that much more.''

"Spoken like a mother, but it still might not be enough,'' Dominique whispered, her heart aching to see him again. Their separation might as well have been a lifetime.

"That's over now. Dr. Canfield gave you a clean bill of health this morning.''

Dominique nodded. "It's the news I've been waiting for. In high school I used to wish I were well endowed, but she told me being smaller breasted had made me the best candidate for this kind of surgery. I pray that's true. If anything does go wrong, and it leaks or encapsulates, I'll have to have another operation.''

"Darling—before the surgery I heard her tell you that those problems only happen in about ten percent of women. Don't look for trouble where there isn't any.''

"I won't. My whole concern is finding the best way to approach Andreas. I'd like to surprise him, but it's very difficult when he's so well protected.''

"Why not just phone him?''

"No. I want him to see me first. You know—catch him off guard. After we're back in Bosnia I'll do some detective work, so he'll never suspect I'm making inquiries.''

"Under the circumstances you'd better hurry and get changed, so we won't be late for the airport.''

Dominique dashed back to the bathroom. She had no intention of missing their flight.

Her hands trembled as she packed her new bikini. The next time she wore it she would be standing in front of her husband. By the look in his eye she would know if he'd lost all desire for her or not. That would tell her if their marriage still had a chance.

Twelve hours later she entered her dad's office at the US consulate in Sarajevo, where she worked for him. The time had come to put her plan into action. Fear and excitement gripped her in spasms.

On the flight from New York she'd come up with the idea to call Andreas's headquarters in Athens from a payphone. She would pretend to be the secretary of a Bosnian importer who wanted to discuss a business venture with him. That way she would find out if he was even in the city.

After opening the morning mail, she decided to slip out while it wasn't busy and make that phone call from the post office, a few buildings down the street.

As she started to get up from the chair, the receptionist buzzed her. "Yes, Walter?"

"There's a Paul Christopoulos here to see you."

The news set her heart tripping like a jackhammer. *Andreas's best friend and personal assistant was out in front?*

Dominique had heard of coincidences, but this one almost caused her to faint. She sank back down in the chair until the lightheaded feeling passed and her skin didn't feel as clammy.

If Paul had come to the consulate in Sarajevo it was for one reason only. Andreas wanted the divorce now, and had sent Paul to negotiate the terms of the settlement.

A year ago she'd demanded Andreas give her a divorce. His only answer had been to put more money in her bank account—money she'd never touched.

Two subsequent demands from her New York attorney had been met with the same silence. She'd quickly learned Andreas had no intention of letting her go, at least on paper. With his wealth and power he was able to write his own rules.

She'd finally given up, realizing his pride hadn't been able to handle her walking out on him. He would give her a divorce when his anger had cooled, not before. But Paul's arrival coming from out of the blue this morning meant she'd waited too long to approach her husband and talk things out.

"Shall I tell him he has to make an appointment? Or are you free to see him now?" Walter prodded, but her mind was miles away.

Andreas must have met a woman.

He was ready to move on with his life. So was Dominique, but she wanted to move forward with her husband by her side.

Placing flattened palms on top of her desk, she said, "Tell him to come in, Walter. Hold any calls for me."

When Paul entered her office, Dominique got up from the chair and walked around her desk to greet him.

He was taller than Andreas, who stood six-three. Both men had powerful builds, but where Paul's hair was reddish brown Andreas's was black.

Loyal, unflappable Paul—the man Andreas trusted like a brother, the man who served as her husband's bodyguard on occasion. To her satisfaction he did a double take before shaking the hand she extended.

Since he'd last seen her she'd undergone a big change in her appearance.

Not only that, a year ago the atmosphere between them had bordered on frigid. But that had been Dominique's fault. Hysterical with pain, she'd left the courthouse before the case against Andreas had gotten under way.

Paul had ridden with her to the airport in an attempt to stop her from leaving Athens before Andreas could talk to her. But in her frantic state she'd been wild with grief, and had informed Paul she was divorcing her husband of four months. That seemed a lifetime ago.

Instead of going back to the seat behind her desk, Dominique rested her hip against the edge and folded her arms. "It's good to see you again, Paul. Sit down. Can I get you something to drink?"

He remained standing. "Nothing for me, Mrs. Stamatakis."

Mrs. Stamatakis. So formal. So correct.

"No one's called me that since I left Athens a year ago." In her shattered condition, the state of her marital status had been no one else's business. Once back with her parents, she'd removed her wedding ring and had insisted on being called by her maiden name.

"You've changed," he murmured unexpectedly.

In other words she wasn't the insecure young woman who'd run from Andreas twelve months ago. Since her agonizing decision to leave her husband, a dramatic transformation had taken place inside and out. The fact that Paul had made such a personal observation to her face meant she'd really knocked him sideways.

It brought a smile to her lips as she contemplated a similar reaction from Andreas, even if he'd finally chosen to divorce her.

But Dominique wasn't about to let that happen. Not yet anyway.

"You haven't changed at all, Paul." He still wore the same austere expression, and those dark-rimmed glasses. Only a year older than Andreas's thirty-three years, Paul seemed older—especially when he was all business, like now.

He didn't reciprocate her smile, but for once in his life she knew her appearance and demeanor had thrown him. That daunting sangfroid of his was missing. She detected the slightest hesitation before he opened his briefcase and pulled out a file.

"Everything's in here." He handed it to her. "You'll find it's an extremely generous offer. After you've read it, all you have to do is write your name on the dotted line and you'll be Ms. Dominique Ainsley again."

Without bothering to open it, she put it back in his briefcase. When she raised up she said, "Before I sign anything I want to see Andreas in person. Where is he?"

Paul studied her speculatively. "On the yacht."

Of course.

It was September, the perfect time to take out the *Cygnus*—the weather was idyllic. "For how long?"

After a pause, "That depends on Olympia."

Her heart plunged to her feet.

So… It appeared Olympia was still the other woman.

The mention of her name touched the deep wound

that had caused Dominique to leave Andreas in the first place. She couldn't help but wonder if Paul had been waiting to reopen it with one thrust of the dagger.

He'd achieved his objective, but nothing he could say would dissuade her from her determination to face her husband and fight for her marriage.

"It doesn't surprise me. Their mutual love for Andreas's sister always made them close." Dominique straightened and walked around her desk. "I presume you came on his private jet?"

Since the answer was obvious, Paul didn't bother to respond. Or maybe he was still surprised that the mention of Olympia hadn't done more damage.

Pretending he'd spoken, she said, "I'll fly back with you."

"Andreas is expecting me to return today."

"Naturally. But that's no problem. My job sends me everywhere, and I always keep my passport with me." And my medicine, she thought automatically.

She pulled her purse from the bottom drawer. Out of the corner of her eye she saw him reach for his cellphone.

"I wouldn't do that if I were you, Paul. I'm still Mrs. Stamatakis, as you reminded me moments ago. Since my husband claimed he would love me forever, you wouldn't want to interfere now, would you?"

Andreas and Paul had grown up in Athens together and were lifetime friends. His allegiance to her husband knew no bounds. But if she wasn't mistaken, shock had caused him to lose a little of his composure—a phenomenon she'd never expected to see.

"This time *I'm* the one asking for your help," she explained. "Would it be too much to expect? I'd like to see Andreas before the sun goes down in the Ionian. Shall we go?''

If he'd picked up on her cryptic remark, he didn't say anything. They passed by Walter's desk in Reception.

"Tell Dad I'm leaving for Greece. By tomorrow morning I'll know my plans and will call him."

The receptionist eyed both of them curiously. "Very good."

Three hours later the helicopter waiting for them at the airport in Athens flew them over the island of Kefalonia.

Dominique's hungry gaze took in its lush green beauty and the golden beaches she'd explored with Andreas. As the helicopter made its descent, the charming little port town of Fiskardo seemed to rise up to greet them. "I don't see the *Cygnus* in the harbor."

"Andreas is sailing from Zakynthos. He wouldn't have expected me to come aboard before late afternoon."

She checked her watch. It was two-thirty p.m. Greek time. "That's good. We can fill a couple of hours shopping with that generous settlement he's planning to give me."

In order to show Paul she meant business, she'd purposely left Sarajevo without going by her parents' house to pack.

Ever the stoic, a quality that meant he had always hidden his disapproval of her as a wife for Andreas, Paul followed her around the stores while she purchased the items she would need for a cruise.

In one of the fitting rooms she removed her tailored

suit and donned a sparkling aqua bikini that had caught her eye. On top of the bikini she put on a tantalizing beach wrap. The white lace affair did nothing to hide what lay beneath.

Sliding into rope sandals, she pulled out the tortoiseshell comb which caught her hair back. After running a brush through the silvery-gold strands, she left it to fall loose to her shoulders from a side part.

When she emerged, Paul's jaw went slack—evidence of his total astonishment. That was twice in one day. It pleased her she could shake Andreas's unshakeable right hand.

Switching her gaze to the water, she saw that the yacht had sailed into the harbor while she'd been in and out of the shops.

Andreas. Her heart pounded outrageously, just imagining her husband's reaction when he saw her.

After a rapid purchase, she hurried toward the launch waiting for them at the pier. The few men in the village, young and old, turned to stare at her. But they didn't call out anything with Paul accompanying her.

It was gratifying to know she could stop traffic, but Andreas was the only male she hoped to rock back on his heels.

One of the crew she recognized from the *Cygnus* sat at the wheel of the tender. When he saw them coming, his wiry figure bounded up on the pier.

"Mrs. Stamatakis—" he cried out in shock when he realized who she was. His eyes rounded until she thought they would pop. Apparently the change in the shy, waif-like wife Andreas had married was astounding.

"Hello, Myron. It's been a long time. How are you?"

"Good." He shot Paul an anxious glance.

"How's your family? Nico must be as tall as you by now." She got into the boat before either man had the presence of mind to assist her.

He muttered something unintelligible, sounding and looking completely unnerved. With Olympia on board the yacht, it was no wonder Myron kept flashing covert signals of distress to Paul. His behavior verified her suspicion that Andreas and Olympia were lovers.

A long time ago Andreas had denied it. Maybe he'd been telling the truth then. But it seemed things had changed in the last year.

"Here." Myron jumped inside after her. Almost as an afterthought he suddenly rushed to hand her a life preserver to put on.

"Thank you."

Clearly he wasn't happy about the situation. No doubt he was hoping Paul would prevent what he viewed as a disaster when Dominique showed up on the yacht. But Paul took a seat, appearing oblivious to the other man's anxiety.

Myron had no choice but to start up the motor and ferry them to the *Cygnus*. In a few minutes she'd climbed the stairs to the top deck. More shocked expressions on the faces of the crew greeted her vision as they discovered her identity.

The yacht was her husband's inner sanctum, and Dominique was invading it.

Too bad.

She was still Mrs. Stamatakis.

The steward finally recovered enough to welcome her aboard. She saw no sign of Andreas or Olympia.

"May I take your things and put them in one of the guest cabins for you?"

"That's all right, Leon. I'll just carry them downstairs to our bedroom."

"But—"

She left him sputtering and walked toward the steps leading to the master bedroom below.

Dominique didn't know what she'd find, but it didn't matter. Over the last year she'd come to realize that her feelings of inadequacy had caused her to run away from Andreas.

He'd needed her during the ugly high-publicity adultery case Olympia's husband had brought against him. Andreas had asked her to trust him. But her emotional scars and immaturity had prevented her from staying the course.

That was why she was here. To tell him how sorry she was that she hadn't believed in their love enough to stand by him and wait for his explanation.

Maybe it was a year too late, but she was ready to hear it now. To give their marriage the chance it deserved.

Her feet had wings as she hurried along the passageway to the master suite where she and Andreas had spent blissful nights together as newlyweds. With her heart thudding in her chest, she knocked on the door. There was no answer. She cautiously turned the handle.

A gasp escaped her throat at discovering the elegant room had been turned into a baby's nursery, complete with a little dresser and changing table. A baby swing had been set up in front of the writing desk.

Her stunned gaze took in the baby blankets strewn on the king-sized bed. Next to it stood a crib with a mobile.

Still in the grip of shock, she put her things on one of the loveseats before tiptoeing over to the little bed.

Pressed up against the bars on his back, sound asleep, lay a dark-haired little boy in a stretchy blue suit.

Andreas's son?

She was too late.

A giant hand squeezed her heart. She couldn't stifle her moan in time. The sound woke up the baby. He took one look at the strange face peering down at him and burst into tears.

"It's okay, sweetheart. It's okay."

The more she tried to assure him, the louder he wailed. His arms and legs moved wildly in the air.

Latent motherly instincts had her reaching for him. He screamed harder and held himself stiff in her arms. She gathered one of the blankets off the bed and rocked him while she paced back and forth. He refused to be comforted.

Suddenly she heard a woman's voice call out. "I'm coming, Ari. I'm coming." The door flew open. Olympia, a dark, voluptuous brunette who was lovelier than ever, rushed inside with a bottle in hand.

But when she saw who was holding her baby she let out a small cry and came to a standstill. Dominique watched the color leave the other woman's face. Evidently she was the last person in the world Olympia had expected to find on board.

If looks could banish, Dominique would be consigned to the other end of the universe right now.

She quickly handed over the baby, who buried his face in his mommy's neck and hugged her with all his might.

"I'm sorry I startled him. When I came down to get settled in I had no idea there was a baby in here. I tried to comfort him, but all I did was alarm him."

Olympia kissed his cheek. Already he was settling down. "Obviously you're looking for Andreas," she murmured, while her unsmiling gaze swept over Dominique. "He's still in Athens, but we're expecting him to join us shortly—aren't we, Ari?"

Us.

No mention of Olympia's husband, Theo. Had he given her a divorce? If so, when?

It appeared Olympia and Andreas had been a family for quite some time. Under the circumstances, why had he waited so long before agreeing to divorce Dominique?

After all the months that she'd been in purgatory for not believing in her husband, it was entirely possible he hadn't been trustworthy from the beginning and she'd been right to leave him.

Her body quaked in pain and confusion, especially since Olympia didn't appear upset or intimidated. Now that the shock had worn off she displayed a certain unmistakable smugness. Even more telling, she didn't try to engage Dominique in conversation.

Anyone watching them would never guess they'd once been friends. At least Dominique had always tried to be friends with her, for Andreas's sake.

Paul had known exactly what he was doing when

he'd let Dominique have her way and come aboard the *Cygnus*. He'd known what she'd find when she burst into the master bedroom.

No doubt Paul had imagined that once Dominique saw the baby she would sign the divorce papers and hightail it back to Sarajevo. He was probably rubbing his hands with glee.

But that was the old Dominique, full of self-doubt.

The new Dominique had come to Greece because she wanted to prove to Andreas that she was a confident woman in her own right—a wife who was his equal in living and loving.

So she would wait until Andreas arrived and they would talk privately. She would listen to what he had to tell her. Once she'd weighed his words, then she would choose to sign the papers or fight for him.

Squaring her shoulders, she said, "Forgive me for intruding, Olympia."

The other woman had seated herself on the bed to hold Ari while he drank from his bottle noisily. "No problem. It was time for him to wake up from his nap anyway. Normally this is the time Andreas plays with him."

Her self-satisfied preoccupation with the baby effectively shut Dominique out. Since it was apparent the other woman had no intention of enlightening her about anything except her closeness to Andreas, Dominique gathered her purse and shopping bags from the loveseat and left the room.

There were guest cabins at the end of the hall closest to the stairs. Dominique entered the one on the right. She deposited her things on the chair.

Instead of succumbing to the urge to curl up in a

ball and sob her heart out, she went up on deck to sunbathe until Andreas arrived. Surely before dark the helicopter from his office building would fly him to Kefalonia? She planted her sunbed so it would be in his direct line of vision when he came aboard.

Paul had kept his promise to the extent that he hadn't alerted Olympia there would be an unexpected visitor coming aboard. But that was before he'd delivered Dominique to the *Cygnus*.

Now that she was ensconced, she imagined he would have phoned her husband almost immediately.

However, if by some fluke Paul had decided to keep the knowledge from Andreas, then the helicopter pilot had probably gossiped to someone who would make sure the news reached the ears of her husband.

But even if Andreas knew she was on board, and was prepared for the physical changes in her, she still wanted to see his expression when they met for the first time after such a painful separation.

She removed her beach cover-up and stretched out. The temperature was in the low eighties. No clouds in the sky. She applied sunscreen to every exposed part of her before lying back.

A few minutes later Leon brought her a sandwich and drink without having asked her if she was hungry. She thanked him for his kindness and proceeded to devour everything.

The seconds passed like seasons while she waited for Andreas. Though the sun finally dropped into the ocean she stayed where she was, not wanting to miss his arrival.

Leon brought her a lemonade and some magazines. He knew her preferences and couldn't have been nicer.

Again she thanked him, then turned over on her stomach to read while there was still enough light. But it was fading fast.

Severely disappointed that Andreas hadn't come yet, she finally got up from the sunbed and went downstairs to shower. On the way she felt drowsy, whether from jet lag or heightened emotions or both, so she lay down on the bed for just a minute to get back her energy.

The next thing she knew, she heard a door close. Then a light went on. Slowly she rolled over to get her bearings.

There was Andreas, standing at the side of the queen-sized bed in a light blue linen business suit. He stared down at her from piercing black eyes set beneath brows as black as raven's wings.

The breath left her body at seeing him in the flesh after all these months.

His dark, handsome face looked leaner, hungrier. She glimpsed shadows in the hollows of his hard-planed cheeks. The cleft in his chin was more pronounced because of his five o'clock shadow, but his sensual mouth was still the same. She thought he'd lost a little weight, but if anything that just made him look more attractive.

Andreas.

She'd missed his arrival—that precious moment she'd been waiting for.

Instead of her catching him off guard on deck, he'd found her crashed on the bed sound asleep, still wearing her bikini. It was embarrassing. She felt foolish.

Her hair was disheveled, and her cheek and legs probably had wrinkles from the quilted comforter. She smelled of sunscreen. Her white skin had picked up too much sun. It felt warm and sticky.

"If you wanted to surprise me, you've succeeded," his deep voice grated, with just a trace of accent.

Dominique slid off the bed and stood up. "No one told you I was here?"

His eyes wandered over her body, but she didn't see so much as a flicker in them to tell her what he was thinking.

"Not until Olympia told me you were down the hall."

Olympia. He'd gone to her first, of course.

Wherever Andreas was, the other woman was never far behind. It had always been thus.

"Where's Paul?"

"Probably in his cabin asleep. It's close to midnight."

"I had no idea it was so late."

"Obviously not." His veiled gaze took in her hair and face. He put his hands on his hips. "Why did you bother to come, Dominique? You're a free woman now. I would have thought you'd never want to step on Greek soil again."

She eyed him frankly. "I didn't sign the papers."

He cocked his dark head. "You want more money? Paul was authorized to give you any sum you requested."

Dominique rubbed her damp palms against her legs. "Money isn't what I'm after."

His body stilled. "What, then? The penthouse in Athens? My villa at Zakynthos? Or do you have an eye on some property I don't know about? Perhaps the *Cygnus*? Name it, and it's yours."

Hearing those words twisted her insides, bringing on excruciating pain. "You know me better than that," she said in a tortured whisper.

There was a chilling twist to his lips. "I thought I did."

"Look, Andreas—" She spread her hands unconsciously. "I can imagine how angry you must have been when I walked out on you—"

She heard his sharp intake of breath. "No. You can't," he responded with quiet savagery. "For a very long time I was so enraged I frightened myself. I wasn't fit company for anyone. But that period is behind me, thank God. If you wanted to impress on me that you're now a whole woman, capable of attracting the attention of every male in sight, the gesture wasn't necessary. To be honest, I preferred the vulnerable young beauty whose violet eyes once looked into mine as if I were her heart and soul. That woman is gone, but I salute the new Ms. Ainsley.

"Whatever you want, tell Paul. I'll send him to you in the morning so you can sign the papers. I hope I've made it clear that I have no desire to see you again. *Yeasas*, Dominique."

CHAPTER TWO

WITH his adrenalin surging, Andreas needed some-
place to go to deal with the force of his chaotic emotions. But the last thing he wanted was members of
his crew speculating on the situation Dominique had
created by appearing like some bewitching ghost from
the past.

Though he'd damned her to hell every day and night
for the last twelve nightmarish months, there was no
denying he was happy for her continuing triumph over
a disease that could have killed her.

There'd been times during their separation when
he'd feared her cancer might have come back, and that
was the reason she hadn't tried to contact him.

When Olympia had informed him she was on board
he'd been incredulous.

After flinging open the guest cabin door, he had still
been disbelieving, seeing the lamplight reveal the gos-
samer gleam of her hair splayed around her like a princess in a fairy tale.

His heart had skipped a dozen beats as he took in
the sight of her beautiful filled-out body lying unconscious on the bed, without her wedding ring, wearing
the kind of bathing suit she wouldn't have been caught
dead in once upon a time.

After being roused from sleep, the picture she'd
made, with those dark-lashed eyes of amethyst fastened on him, was indelibly impressed in his mind.

Damn you, Paul.

Anger drove him down the hall to the other man's cabin. He rapped on the door.

"Come in. I've been expecting you."

Paul was seated at a table, doing some work on his laptop. He removed his glasses and looked across the room at Andreas, who shut the door before leaning against it.

He understood Paul well enough to know the other man hadn't approved of his marriage to Dominique, though he'd never said the words aloud. Paul didn't have to. They read each other easily—or so Andreas had thought.

"How come she's on board, Paul?"

"She's still your wife and she asked for my loyalty."

Struggling for breath, Andreas advanced toward him. "What made you give it?"

"After you ignored her wishes for a divorce, it seemed a small thing to grant."

Andreas's mouth tightened. "There were consequences. Olympia found her holding Ari."

Paul shut the laptop. "Since you're divorcing Dominique, what difference does it make?"

Damn you again.

"First thing in the morning I want the papers signed and her escorted off the yacht. When she's gone, bring them to me. Is that too much to ask?"

His friend eyed him critically before he said, "No."

Long after Andreas had disappeared, Dominique could still feel the cabin sizzle with the white-hot heat of his fury.

She ran to the shower and turned it on full blast. Hopefully no one would be able to hear her initial paroxysm of tears. They'd blend with the stream of water.

Once she'd washed her hair, she toweled off and slipped on the robe she'd purchased. Wide awake and restless, she found herself at the porthole, staring blindly at the water.

Andreas had found no pleasure in looking at her tonight. His mind's eye had been searching for the old Dominique he'd rescued after a freak accident in front of his villa on Zakynthos.

Twenty-six months ago she'd just finished her junior year at New York University, and had gone into the clinic for a routine checkup and mammogram. It had revealed she had cancer. Immediately she'd undergone surgery, followed by chemo and radiation therapy.

When she'd been well enough to travel, she and her mom had joined her father in Sarajevo, where he worked for the US state department.

It was there she'd begun a vigorous program of physical exercise to get strong. She'd built up until she could run organized marathons in Bosnia and Greece.

When she'd heard about the annual 15k marathon on Zakynthos Island, in the Ionian Sea, she had decided to enter it. But it had been against her parents' wishes. She was five feet five and then only ninety-five pounds. The doctor had told her she needed to put on weight so she wouldn't endanger her ability to have children one day.

Her parents had worried about her so much, she'd

promised that after the race was over she'd cut down on her running and concentrate on gaining weight.

She'd flown to Zakynthos with a couple of her runner friends and they'd begun the race. Halfway through, the route had run past a walled private area of the island. As Dominique had rounded a bend in the road, a truck had come out of nowhere and side-swiped her, knocking her unconscious.

Andreas had witnessed the accident. He was the one who'd carried her into his villa and had called for the doctor. In order to stop more bleeding, his hands had removed the torn and bloodied T-shirt and sports bra with its prosthesis.

When she'd come to, her eyes had beheld the most handsome Greek man she'd ever seen in her life. His black gaze had been so incredibly tender as he'd smiled down into her eyes and assured her she was safe. It hadn't dawned on her he'd seen the scar of her mastectomy. Not until after the doctor's examination had she learned from Andreas that he was the one who'd rescued her.

She couldn't understand how he'd been able to look at her as if she brought him pleasure when she'd lost the headscarf which covered her pathetic two-inch growth of hair. Since her last chemo treatment it had taken a long time for it to start coming back in.

He was a big, powerful man, at least two hundred pounds of rock-hard muscle. She was a slip of girl, half his weight. And she'd been bloody and scruffy and she'd wanted to disappear because she was so embarrassed by his relentless attention to her every need.

Before she knew how it had happened, he'd invited her parents to be his guests for the next few days, until she'd recovered from her concussion and was well enough to go back to Sarajevo. Even then he'd insisted they fly on his private jet to Athens before transferring to his helicopter.

No sooner had she returned to her parents' house, than Andreas had flown to Sarajevo—that evening. Her mom had invited him to stay over. What should have been one night turned into a week. Her parents had been enchanted by him.

Dominique had worshipped him in her heart. He was bigger than life. His business interests had made his name famous all over Greece. Ten years older than she was, experienced, sophisticated—he'd been as out of reach to her as the nearest planet.

Despite her protestations that her cancer could come back at any time, he'd told her it didn't matter. A few months later they were married, in his family's church in Athens. At the altar he'd whispered that they would live all the years God gave them, and rejoice.

Though his parents had come to the wedding, Dominique had received a cool reception from them. Andreas had explained they were still grieving for their daughter Maris, who'd been killed in a tragic car accident two years earlier. The shock had almost been too much for them.

He'd told Dominique not to be concerned. When they'd passed through the worst of their mourning period they would embrace her into the family. She had accepted his explanation, but inside she couldn't help blaming herself. Dominique thought it was *she* they didn't like. She'd been hurt by their lack of enthusiasm over the wedding festivities.

Immediately after, Dominique and Andreas had

spent the months of May and June on the *Cygnus* enjoying a lengthy honeymoon. Nights of lovemaking she could never have imagined.

Andreas was a tender lover who could be a great tease. After a night of rapture he would tempt her with calorie-laden foods. He wanted a baby, so it was necessary to fatten her up.

Sometimes he invited Olympia and Theo Panos, recently married, to join them. Andreas's friendship with Olympia went back a long way because she'd been best friends with Maris from childhood, and Andreas felt a loyalty to his late sister's best friend.

Since Andreas seemed to find pleasure being around Olympia, because of her connection to his only sister, Dominique had encouraged him to invite the couple for the occasional weekend. Theo, a contemporary of Andreas, ran a successful textile company and was always a very entertaining guest. Dominique liked him a lot.

Olympia was friendly enough to Dominique in front of their husbands, but she never exuded the kind of warmth that would have turned them into friends on their own.

In private, she'd told Dominique before the wedding that Theo thought it very courageous of Andreas to marry her. According to him, not all men could have handled Dominique's problem.

At the time Dominique had refused to let Olympia's comment sting because she was so gloriously happy. In fact she'd felt ashamed that she'd ever fallen into that terrible state of feeling sorry for herself because she'd been diagnosed with cancer.

If it hadn't been for the disease she would never

have started running marathons, would never have been rescued by the man she loved to the last atom of her being.

The honeymoon had continued when they returned to Zakynthos. Then had come August, when Andreas had to get back to work. They'd left for Athens and there her happiness had slowly been crushed, until there had been nothing left of their marriage.

One evening Andreas had called her from work and told her he wouldn't be home until the next day. To her surprise he hadn't confided the reason why.

For the next two weeks when he joined her in bed, after she'd gone to sleep waiting for him, his love-making had become more primitive. Yet he wouldn't tell her what was going on in his life to change him so drastically. All he'd asked her to do was trust him.

One night she hadn't been able to stand the suspense any longer and had demanded to know what was wrong.

He'd levered himself from the bed and stared down at her. "I've wanted to protect you, but you have a right to know that Theo has brought a lawsuit against me."

What? With her heart skidding to a stop, she got to her knees and looked up at him. "Why on earth would he do that when you're such good friends?"

Andreas's mouth tightened. "No. We've never been good friends. He's always been jealous of my relationship with Olympia. Now he's charging the two of us with adultery."

The blood pounded in her ears. "Why does he feel so threatened?" She couldn't disguise the tremor in her voice.

He studied her features for a long time. "Because he found us together at my flat a few weeks ago."

She felt her heart die. "What flat?" she whispered.

"I keep one in the Plaka, for business contacts when they have to stay over."

"And you never told me?"

"I didn't intentionally keep it a secret from you, Dominique. The truth is I have flats in various places in Greece for when I travel on business."

When she groaned at this oversight he dismissed as unimportant, he said, "The situation with Olympia isn't what Theo thinks. I swear it. But I can't talk about it yet. You know I love you." He reached for her and crushed her in his arms. "It's until death, *agape mou.*"

Yes, she knew he loved her. She also knew a lot of men who had wives they loved and mistresses they enjoyed on the side.

Olympia was seven years older than Dominique. Beautiful, full-figured, strong-willed. Dominique sensed she'd hero-worshipped Andreas for years. The attraction had probably been there since Olympia's early teens, when her relationship with Maris had thrown her into Andreas's company.

Yet reason told her that if he'd wanted to marry Olympia he would have done so, before Dominique had ever run in a marathon that happened to pass by his villa.

So what had happened to change him? Had he discovered too late that Dominique's disfigurement was a turn-off? Was it pity he'd ended up feeling for her, and he'd waited to give her a divorce until he felt she could handle it?

Maybe he'd found her so lacking physically he'd discovered Olympia was the woman he should have married after all.

It took no imagination to understand why Andreas had sought the other woman out when he wanted a change from his child bride, who some people mistook for a boy from a distance.

Dominique turned away from the porthole.

She might no longer be his waif-like bride, but she was still his wife. If pity wasn't the reason he'd taken so long to give her a divorce, maybe it had more to do with Theo. Maybe Andreas had been waiting for Theo to grant Olympia her freedom first. Theo was a proud Greek too.

In pain at the trial, he might have decided to make his wife suffer by exposing her affair with Andreas yet still keeping her bound to him. If Ari was Andreas's son, then Theo's pain would have made him crazy for a while.

Dominique couldn't pretend she wasn't shocked by the child's existence, but she'd come back to Greece to ask her husband's forgiveness for not trusting him.

If she were to run away now, and not give Andreas a chance to explain why Olympia and Ari were installed in the bedroom Dominique had once shared with him, then she'd learned nothing over the past year.

Determined that this time she would fight fire with grit, she climbed under the covers, willing oblivion to come.

At some point the phone rang by her bed, jerking her from a sound sleep. She was surprised to discover it was morning. Only one person would be calling her, and it wouldn't be Andreas.

Still, her heart raced as she picked up the receiver. "Hello?"

"It's Paul. May I come by your room?"

"Of course."

"I'll be there in five minutes."

Dominique scrambled out of bed to get dressed. She quickly put on new lingerie and slipped into a pair of khaki shorts and a sleeveless cotton top in a plum color.

By the time she heard his knock she'd run a brush through her hair and applied a pink frost lipstick.

"Come in, Paul." She held the door open for him. He'd shown up with the file he'd pulled from his brief-case yesterday morning. "Why don't you sit down at the table?"

Without waiting for his reply she started packing things in shopping bags. She felt his eyes on her. When he didn't say anything, she took the initiative.

"I'll make this easy for you. Andreas needed time before he was ready to grant me a divorce. Now I've discovered I need time to think about it, so I'm not going to sign anything yet."

"I figured as much when you didn't act on it in Sarajevo."

She nodded. "Andreas told me I could have whatever I wanted, be it money or one of his properties. So until further notice I'll be staying at the villa on Zakynthos."

Andreas would be furious. Hopefully he would follow her there, where they could talk in private.

"If you'll arrange for the helicopter to pick me up, I'm ready to go now."

"It's waiting for you."

Naturally. Andreas had said he wanted her gone this morning.

Paul got to his feet. "You don't want breakfast first?"

"No. I'll worry about eating later."

She reached for her things and walked out the door. Paul followed closely behind.

All was quiet as they climbed to the top deck. It was only seven-thirty a.m.—the beginning of another beautiful day. She made her way to the port side, where she could see the launch bobbing up and down in the cobalt blue water.

As she reached the bottom step Paul took her bags while Myron greeted her and assisted her into the tender. After handing her a life preserver he started the motor, and they headed for the shore in the near distance.

When they arrived at the pier Paul was kind enough to take her bags and walk to the helicopter with her.

Dominique refused to look back. From now on her motto was to forge ahead without entertaining negative thoughts, no matter if it killed her. She'd learned a lot in her battle with cancer.

There had been a time when she hadn't thought she'd even be alive today. But by some miracle she'd survived those months of chemo—months she wanted to forget, because her body had been so drained and weak she hadn't been able to lift her head off the pillow.

Now she was strong and healthy again, ready to

fight another kind of battle that would test her emotional mettle.

As she turned to thank Paul, he surprised her by climbing inside after her.

"I'll be fine from here. Andreas will be waiting for you."

He strapped himself in the seat behind the pilot. "I'll accompany you to make certain there's no problem."

For some reason he was going out of his way to help her. She didn't understand it, but she was grateful for it and had no right to question his agenda.

"Thank you very much."

She proceeded to take her place in the co-pilot's seat. Once she'd buckled up, the rotors whirred and she felt the helicopter rise into the balmy air.

Soon the yacht was only a tiny speck in the ocean of blue. She experienced a sharp pain at realizing she was flying away from Andreas once more. But this time it wasn't out of his life. Not yet. Hopefully never.

With a feeling of *déjà vu* she found herself gazing out over the familiar scenery below on their flight south to Zakynthos, one of the largest islands in the Ionian. Before long it came into view.

Andreas had once told her that the Venetians, who'd ruled it for three hundred years, called it the flower of the orient. She could see why—especially from the air.

The eastern side was lushly vegetated, with many fertile groves of olive and citrus trees spreading to incredibly sandy beaches. The mountains on the western side, with their high-walled white cliffs, swooped down to the sea.

Andreas's modern white villa lay hidden in the

sparsely populated region to the north, where the steepest cliffs gave out on a breathtaking vista of Shipwreck Beach, with its crystal blue waters.

Soon she could make out the estate and the oval swimming pool. Dominique marveled at the pilot's ability to set them down on the landing pad with the precision of an eagle coming to rest on a mountain crag.

She turned to Paul, who'd jumped down behind her to give her the bags. "I'm aware you've gone against Andreas's wishes by helping me. Thank you for being my friend, even though it goes against your instincts."

There was a moment where she sensed he wanted to say something, then thought better of it. She would have urged Paul to speak his mind, but she couldn't with the pilot there.

In the distance she could see Eleni, the family retainer in charge of Andreas's staff at the villa. She'd emerged from the east entrance of the house, spry as ever despite her advanced years.

Dominique started walking toward her. A little closer, the gray-haired woman recognized Dominique. Her hands flew to her face in surprise. She made a sound of surprise.

"Good morning, Eleni. How are you?"

"Kyrie Stamatakis didn't tell me you were coming."

"He doesn't know yet, but it's all right. Paul brought me."

She stared at Dominique. "You look different."

"Not exactly like the injured marathon runner you nursed a long time ago? I've never forgotten your kindness to me, especially during those first few days.''

A softness entered the older woman's expression. ''You were sick after your accident.''

''Not anymore.''

''The cancer has stayed away?''

Dominique nodded. ''Hopefully for good.''

The older woman's eyes grew suspiciously bright. ''How long will you be here?''

''I'm not sure yet.''

At that point Paul said something to her in Greek. Dominique had learned some elements of the language, but she couldn't follow their rapid conversation.

Whatever transpired, Eleni didn't ask any more questions. She simply took the shopping bags from her and said, ''Come with me.'' The emotion in her voice warmed Dominique's heart.

''I'll put you in the blue room where Kyrie Stamatakis carried you after your accident on the road.''

If that was Eleni's subtle way of shielding Dominique from any unpleasant surprises in the master bedroom, like more evidence of Olympia and Ari, then Dominique was grateful for that small mercy.

She and Paul followed the housekeeper inside the home where she'd known such great happiness with Andreas. It was here they'd fallen in love.

Maybe this was a doomed mission. But if she'd faced cancer with such a negative outlook she would never have survived. Hopefully in this ambience Andreas would come to her and let go of his anger long enough to really talk to her. Right now that was all she could hope to expect.

"Is there anything else I can do for you before I leave for Athens?"

Dominique swung around to face Paul. "You're not going straight back to the yacht?"

"No. I have business to attend to."

"So do I. Could I fly with you?"

He blinked. "You want to go there today?"

"Yes."

Before any more time passed Dominique wanted clarification on several vital points. Theo was the only person who could answer those questions for her.

"Just allow me to change into something suitable."

"Of course."

She didn't require Eleni's help to find the blue room. As soon as she was alone she put on the white sundress with *café-au-lait* swirls she'd purchased the day before. When she looked in the mirror, she noted with satisfaction that the sun she'd picked up yesterday had made an improvement in her coloring.

After joining Paul in the foyer, she turned to Eleni. "Depending on how long it takes me, I'll be back tonight or tomorrow."

"Very good."

"Let's go, Paul."

Andreas frowned when he glanced at his watch. It was noon. Paul should have reported to him by now. He got up from the desk in his study and walked down the hall to his friend's stateroom.

When he didn't answer the door, Andreas concluded Dominique was being difficult. It wasn't like Paul to let any problem stand in his way. If it was taking this long, then he needed help—something Andreas never imagined would happen.

Though he hadn't intended to see Dominique again, he feared she might still be in her room, hammering out the details of the divorce settlement with Paul.

His features grim, Andreas headed for her cabin, steeling himself not to react to the sight of her. Without bothering to knock, he let himself inside.

No one was there.

The bed was still unmade—evidence of where she'd spent the night. He fought the image of her lying in it, all that warm femininity he'd been denied for the last year.

Where were they?

As he turned to leave, his gaze fastened on the manila legal file lying on the table in the corner. He reached for it and seized the papers inside.

She still hadn't signed them.

Paul was nowhere around.

Sucking in his breath, he headed for his study, where he'd left his cellphone. The pilot would tell him what he wanted to know.

In a minute he heard the other man say, "First I flew her to Zakynthos."

First?

Andreas swore softly.

"Where's Paul?"

"Mr. Christopoulos flew on to Athens. At the last minute Mrs. Stamatakis decided to go with him."

He grimaced. "Did you put them down at the airport?"

"No. Your office building. She said she had business in the city."

What business?

His jaw hardened. "I see. Fly back to Fiskardo and pick me up. I'll be waiting for you."

"Yes, sir."

He pocketed his phone, gathered the file, and went up on deck to find Olympia. She was sitting on the edge of a sunbed watching Ari, who was lying on a quilt while he played with some toys.

Normally Andreas would have hunkered down to tickle him, but the news that Dominique hadn't left Greece had come as a stunning surprise.

Olympia eyed him expectantly. "Did she sign the divorce papers?"

He gazed out over the water with unseeing eyes. "No." Her mystifying behavior had him completely baffled.

"I think I know why."

"Then you know a hell of a lot more than I do." His hands formed fists.

"When she asked you for a divorce she made it clear she didn't want a financial settlement, but I believe something has happened to change her mind."

"Like what?" Andreas questioned.

"For one thing it's obvious she's undergone reconstructive surgery, which is a huge expense.

"For another, having contracted cancer so early in her life, I'm sure her doctor has told her it's more than possible it's going to come back. For all we know her physician may have suggested she have another mastectomy as a preventative measure. She may need more money for that."

Andreas cringed, because Olympia had just touched on the one area that filled him with terror.

"If the cancer spreads, it's inevitable she'll be facing more battles in the future. When you think about it, her hospital bills could end up being enormous."

Bile rose in his throat.

"We both know she's not a mercenary person, and would never beg you for anything. She has too much pride for that—otherwise she wouldn't have left the courtroom without hearing any testimony. Her abandonment of you reveals an immaturity which shouldn't have surprised you, considering her young age."

Dominique had abandoned him all right. The memory of it ate at him like a corrosive acid.

"But I'm thinking that now you've finally decided to give her the divorce, she's panicked. After looking ahead at the years to come, she probably decided to fly here in order to ensure there'll be some kind of a medical fund set up for her care. Just think if she has to go into the hospital over and over throughout her life, for chemo treatments or more surgery."

Haunted by the thought, Andreas's mind flooded with memories of last night, when he'd told her he never wanted to see her again. What if Olympia was right and Dominique was facing more surgery, but hadn't been able to bring herself to tell him?

"I recall her mentioning how much she hated being a burden on her parents," Olympia continued, unaware of the tremendous upheaval going on inside him. "With her father a salaried government employee, it only makes sense she would seek you out for financial help, even though she didn't think about that when she first asked for the divorce. But a year has gone by, and with it probably more surgery. No doubt paying more doctor bills has forced her to ponder her precarious position.''

''I don't want to talk about it anymore.''

''Of course not. But to remain in denial won't make the truth go away, Andreas. She always was a quiet little thing. It's probably very hard for her to talk about her cancer with you.''

Olympia understood a lot more than Andreas had given her credit for. Dominique had always shut him out when it came to the subject of her health. He'd had to tread carefully in order not to make her retreat inside herself.

But those days were over.

Seeing her again had left him reeling. It was time to act on his feelings before his agony reached its zenith.

''I'm flying to Athens.''

''You can look for her, but you won't find her if she doesn't want to be found,'' Olympia reminded him. ''Why not stay on the yacht with me and wait? She'll be back when she's ready. You know how timid she is. She's probably hiding somewhere while she musters up the courage to approach you again.''

''I've done enough waiting,'' he ground out. Olympia had always been on his side, but, so help him, he couldn't think, let alone talk right now.

In the next breath he'd phoned Myron and alerted him he needed to go ashore.

Once the launch had ferried him to the pier, he phoned Paul. All he got was his voicemail. Cursing under his breath, he walked to the village and grabbed a cup of coffee while he waited for the chopper.

As he was draining the last of it, his cellphone rang. He checked the caller ID and clicked on.

"What in the name of heaven happened, Paul?" he thundered.

"Over the years I've been willing to do anything for you, Andreas. But when it comes to your wife you ask too much. If you want to fire me, go ahead."

His hand tightened on the phone. "Where is she?" he demanded.

"I have no idea."

"Did she appear ill to you?"

"Ill?" There was a long silence. "No. But you know she's a master at hiding anything of a personal nature."

Andreas took a deep breath. "It was your job to find out what business she had in Athens!"

"I'm not her husband."

His head reared. "How did Dominique get to you?"

"Probably the same way she got to you."

Andreas heard the click.

He stood there frozen.

Paul's silence on the subject of Dominique had always puzzled him. Long ago he'd decided his friend doubted her suitability as a wife for Andreas by virtue of the ten-year difference in their ages and her being of a different nationality. But his uncharacteristic behavior since flying to Sarajevo had dispelled that myth. In fact Paul's willingness to risk saying something that could hurt their lifetime friendship was a revelation.

If he didn't know better, Andreas could be forgiven for thinking his friend harbored secret feelings for Dominique.

While he grappled with a dichotomy of emotions, the helicopter came into view. Andreas paid for his coffee, then stepped off the terrace of the taverna into the sun.

His mood fierce since talking to Olympia, he scarcely noticed the flight to the landing pad atop his office building in Athens.

"Did Mrs. Stamatakis tell you what her plans were?"

"No, sir. You would have to ask Mr. Christopoulos."

"If she calls you for any reason I want to be informed," he told his pilot.

The other man nodded.

In a few minutes Andreas had called his driver once again. "Take me to the villa."

If Olympia was right, and Dominique had gone there to gather her courage before returning to the yacht, he would save her the trouble.

Before this hour was up there was going to be a confrontation. He would force her to deal with the one painful issue they'd both avoided discussing from the beginning of their relationship.

CHAPTER THREE

PANOS TEXTILES was situated near Syntagma Square, where the Stamatakis office building was also located. Dominique paid the taxi driver and hurried inside the ground floor, where a receptionist greeted her. She was going to see Olympia's husband—or ex-husband, as he seemed to be now.

"I'd like to see Theo Panos, if he's here."

"Do you have an appointment?"

"No. If I could please speak to his secretary?"

"What's your name?"

"Dominique Stamatakis."

The mere mention of Andreas's name caused the woman's eyes to widen before she spoke into the phone. A rapid conversation in Greek ensued. In a few minutes Dominique was cleared to go up to the top floor.

When she emerged from the elevator Theo himself was waiting for her. He too was dark-haired, like Andreas, though not quite as tall or hard-muscled. She thought him quite attractive in white slacks and a light olive jacket with a darker green shirt.

He studied her at some length, his expression sober. "The butterfly has broken out of her chrysalis. You look very, very beautiful, Dominique."

"Thank you, Theo. I appreciate your willingness to see me on such short notice."

"I never thought to lay eyes on you again. Come

in to my private office where we can talk without interruption.''

When he'd shown her through the suite to a comfortable leather seat opposite his desk, she said, ''There was a time when I couldn't imagine myself returning to Greece for any reason.''

He walked over to the bar. ''Sherry?'' he asked, lifting a bottle.

''Nothing for me.''

''Not even Perrier water?''

''No, thank you.''

Taking her at her word, he carried a small glass of retsina to his desk and sat down. She watched him take a few swallows.

''All right. Now tell me why you've entered enemy territory. Does your husband know you've come to my office?''

''No. This is strictly my own idea.''

Theo sat back. ''Go on.''

''I'm here to learn the status of your marriage to Olympia.''

Her question must have shocked him because his brows met in a distinct frown. ''You don't know?''

She shook her head. ''I left the courtroom after the opening statement at the trial and went straight to the airport to book my flight to Sarajevo. I never knew the outcome of the trial. I didn't want to know anything. Once I was back with my parents, my attorney drew up divorce papers and sent them to Andreas on several occasions. But he never signed them.''

''All this time he has refused you a divorce?'' Theo sounded incredulous.

''Until two days ago, when he sent Paul to Sarajevo.

It seems he now wants to be free. I decided to fly back with Paul and have a meeting with Andreas before I signed anything. To my surprise I found Olympia on board the *Cygnus* with a little baby. She made no explanations or excuses. In fact she didn't say anything except that she was expecting Andreas back from Athens shortly. That's why I decided to come to you, to learn the truth of the situation."

He leaned forward. "You would believe me after I ruined your husband's reputation in court?"

She wanted answers, but wasn't prepared for his blunt speaking.

"Yes. I always believed you and I were friends. As horrible as I thought it was to make everything public, I think you must have loved Olympia a great deal to have been in that much pain. Please, Theo—tell me what's going on?"

Lines marred his features. "I haven't seen Olympia for months, so I have no idea. If you're talking about the trial, neither she or Andreas admitted to an affair. She testified that she'd been shopping in the Plaka and became ill. Because I was out of town she called Andreas, who told her to go to his nearby flat and wait for him. What she didn't know was that I had lied about being away. Without her realizing it, I followed her that day and caught them together. She was in his bed.

"The judge heard my testimony and didn't buy the weak excuse either. In the end he granted me a divorce. Olympia's been a free agent ever since."

Dominique was the one in shock now. If Olympia had been divorced for a year, why had it taken Andreas so long to decide he wanted his freedom?

She searched his aristocratic features. "Did you know Olympia was pregnant at the time?"

"Yes."

Gearing up her courage she asked, "Whose son is Ari?"

"Mine," Theo answered baldly. "After the baby was born, a DNA test was done, confirming I was the father."

The unexpected revelation swept through Dominique, leaving her limp with relief. She bit her lip. "If that's true, is there any possibil—?"

"None!" he declared, with enough force that she believed him. "With hindsight I realized Olympia had married me because she couldn't have Andreas. From early on it was clear that she had deep feelings for him. Though she'd always denied any involvement with him, I never believed her. Finally I got the proof."

Andreas had always admitted Theo had found them together.

It isn't what Theo thinks, he'd said.

Dominique struggled for breath. What if it really hadn't been what it looked like and there was another explanation?

"Your husband tried to defend the situation by telling the court she'd been attacked by food poisoning, but I know what I saw. My wife never looked healthier," he muttered. "Since it isn't in me to spend the rest of my life living a travesty of a marriage, I took them to court. Because news of the pregnancy came out during the trial, and paternity couldn't be proven until the baby was delivered, the judge came down on my side and only granted Olympia a modest monthly sum in the final divorce decree.''

"I see. What about Andreas?''

"I didn't demand monetary compensation from him, if that's what you mean. The damage to his reputation was enough.''

Dominique shivered. He sounded so cold-blooded, but she had to remember what he'd been through.

If she had jumped to conclusions over what Andreas had said about Theo finding them at the apartment together, she could just imagine how Theo had felt.

To see his wife in another man's bed, especially when that man was a good friend, had to have shattered him. No wonder he'd felt completely betrayed.

"I don't blame you for thinking the worst, Theo.''

"Thank you, Dominique. If you want to know, I've applauded you for your strength in staying away from Andreas. After what you've been through, with your illness, you're too good a person to be taken for granted.''

"According to Olympia, you thought it was courageous of him to marry me in the first place.''

A look of unfeigned surprise broke out on his face. "Courageous?''

"That's what Olympia told me you'd said.''

"Then she lied to you. She's good at that.''

Dominique groaned.

Theo eyed her frankly. "The only comment I ever made was that I thought Andreas a luckier man than he knew to have met you.''

Somehow Dominique believed him. "Thank you.''

"You're welcome.''

"But you have to admit you thought I was a little mouse of a wife?"

The first smile she'd seen broke at the corner of his mouth. "More a lovely, endangered baby bird who needed protecting."

It was an apt description.

She *had* been like a nervous little bird. Paranoid that Andreas's interest would eventually wear off, uncertain of herself in his sophisticated world of friends and business contacts, frightened of Olympia's place in Andreas's life, worried her cancer would come back, fearful she might not be able to give him a child or live long enough to be a proper wife. The list went on and on.

"I'm sorry you were hurt so badly, Theo. Since you and Olympia share a child, it must be hard to work out visitation."

He shook his head. "I gave up my parental rights to him."

"What?"

"Don't look so horrified. After the trial, she informed me that as soon as you and Andreas were divorced they were planning to be married and Andreas would be raising Ari."

No wonder Olympia had paled when she'd caught Dominique in the stateroom holding Ari. If she and Andreas were on the verge of getting married, the last thing she would want was trouble from Dominique.

"For six months I lived with the assumption that the baby was Andreas's child. By the time he was born and I received the DNA results learning he was my son, I decided it was best to leave it all alone."

The room tilted for a moment. She clung to the

armrests of her chair. "That's tragic! You're a wonderful person. I can't bear it that your son won't ever know you."

He stared at her mournfully. "Andreas has been Ari's father since the day he took Olympia and the baby home from the hospital. I'm not up to a lifetime of battles."

"You could live to regret that decision, Theo," she cried.

"Perhaps. But I hope to marry again. Next time I'll choose a gentle creature like you, who will love only me and give me a son or a daughter."

He studied her for a brief moment. "Andreas had it all and didn't even know it. What a fool he is."

Theo was still in a state of complete denial about his feelings for Olympia and the baby. Dominique sensed his pain. Something wasn't right here.

If Dominique didn't have that talk with Andreas soon, she was going to explode.

"Thank you for answering my questions, Theo. I wish you well. I really do."

"I want your happiness too."

She got up from the chair on shaky legs. He hurried around his desk and cupped her elbow to escort her out of the office to the elevator.

"How long will you be in Greece?"

"I'm not sure." More than ever she needed time alone with Andreas, away from Olympia.

"For old times' sake, would you allow me to take you out to dinner tonight at Zorba's?"

"I'd like that a lot, but I'm still not divorced."

Since the trial, Dominique had learned to avoid the appearance of evil. If a journalist were to catch them dining at the famous restaurant, where the four of them had eaten after they'd come home from their honeymoon, it would create more adverse sensationalism for Andreas in the press.

She couldn't help but wonder how much damage the bad publicity from the trial had already done to his business interests, let alone his personal life.

After a silence, "You're a rare breed of woman, Dominique. Whatever possessed Andreas to treat you in such a cavalier manner is beyond my comprehension. Good luck to you, my dear."

He kissed her cheek.

The last thing she saw was the glint of pain in his eyes before the elevator door closed. It haunted her all the way to the airport, where she took a commercial helicopter back to Zakynthos.

She could have returned to Andreas's office building and taken his private helicopter, but she'd already created a minor sensation by showing up there with Paul earlier. In order to minimize the gossip, she thought it wise to keep the rest of her agenda private.

The moment she returned to the villa, Eleni fluttered around to make her comfortable. While Dominique did laps in the pool, to release her nervous energy, the housekeeper brought her dinner and put it on the patio table.

After an exhausting workout, Dominique climbed out of the water and wrapped her hair in a towel before seating herself. It seemed the cook had outdone herself, preparing Dominique's favorite seafood salad and buttered rolls.

Because the exercise had whipped up her appetite, she ate everything in sight. While she was finishing off a second cup of coffee, she heard the telltale sound of a helicopter approaching.

Her heart thudded unmercifully hard.

Was it Paul, on another mission from Andreas? Or had her husband decided to take matters into his own hands and get rid of her himself before the night was out?

Maybe he'd brought Olympia and the baby with him.

Though she was almost jumping out of her skin, Dominique forced herself to remain at the table and wait.

At the first sight of Andreas's arresting features and tall, well-honed physique, in beige trousers and a white crew neck sport shirt, her body melted with desire.

He had the most beautiful olive complexion she'd ever seen. The twilight brought out lines of experience around the mouth which used to kiss her with such passion she could hardly breathe just thinking about it.

Gazing at the combination of black eyes, and hair with a tendency to curl, she marveled that he'd once chosen to marry her when he could have had any woman he wanted.

If he'd brought Olympia with him she was nowhere in sight.

He approached the table. His strong, suntanned fingers curled around the back of the chair opposite her.

"Exactly where did you go today?" he demanded.

"I needed to visit someone."

"But you didn't tell Paul?"

"It wasn't his business."

His eyes smoldered in anger. "Anyone I know?"

"Does it matter?"

"Dominique!" His harsh tone caused her to flinch. "Did you have to see a doctor?"

"No—" she cried, bewildered by the question.

"Don't lie to me."

"I'm not. I had a checkup in New York before I came to Greece. If you don't believe me, call Dr. Canfield."

She could hear his mind working. "If that's true, then there's only one person I can imagine you going to see. It was Theo, wasn't it?"

Dominique colored.

"I can see in your face I'm right." He shook his head. "Don't you realize what you've done?"

"What's so terrible about it? I decided to talk to the one person who could give me some answers."

"So you appealed to my arch enemy instead of me?"

'Oh, really, Andreas!" She made an exasperated gesture. "Since you made it clear it was goodbye last night, I had no choice but to go to the one person who knew what happened at the trial."

"My attorney sent yours a full transcript."

"I know, but I could never bring myself to read it."

Muttering a curse, he pressed a balled fist to his forehead. She stared at him, suddenly conscious of the towel still wrapped around her head. In a jerky motion she pulled it off.

His glittering black eyes wandered to the damp hair she didn't bother to rearrange. "Yet you decided you could believe every word Theo told you instead of coming to your own husband?" He was furious.

She hunched her shoulders. "With Olympia and the baby on board, the *Cygnus* didn't seem the place to have a private talk with you."

He swore again and paced restlessly about the patio. "Did he tell you Ari was my flesh and blood?"

"As a matter of fact he didn't."

Andreas halted and stared at her with a brooding gaze. "And you accepted that as the truth?"

"Yes."

"But when I asked you to trust me you couldn't do it." His eyes had grown bleak as the dead of winter.

Dominique just sat there and studied him helplessly. It had been a whole year, and she loved him so desperately. Yet here they were, almost at each other's throats. A small sob escaped.

She finally found her voice. "That was a long time ago."

He looked at her grimly. "So long, in fact, you appealed to *him*, not to me."

She heaved a sigh. Somehow this conversation had turned into a slanging match—the last thing she'd wanted to happen.

"On the yacht you told me you never wanted to see me again." She struggled for breath. "I went down the only avenue left open to me."

He let out a frustrated groan. It sent shivers across her skin because she didn't know how to interpret it.

"So now you assume you know the truth?" he bit out.

She put a hand to her throat. "Please, Andreas— can we get off the subject of Theo for a minute? Th— There's something I have to ask you."

His face closed up. "I already know what it is. You

don't have to beg me to pay for your medical expenses, Dominique. Don't you realize I would never leave you destitute?''

What was he talking about?

''Admit that's what you want spelled out in the divorce papers before signing them. What I don't understand is why you didn't tell me that last night. Paul could have redone them right there.''

Her nails dug into the palms of her hands. ''I'm not here because of unpaid medical bills! Where is this coming from, Andreas? My insurance has paid for everything and it always will.''

A stillness swirled around him. ''Then what have I missed?''

''When Paul showed up at the consulate I realized you were ready to give me a divorce. D-Does that mean you're going to marry Olympia?'' she stammered.

His jaw hardened. ''If I tell you yes, does that mean I can expect to wait as long for my freedom as I forced you to wait for yours?''

''That's a cruel question to ask—'' she cried.

''You taught me the meaning of the word,'' he answered with wilting contempt.

''*Andreas*—'' she tried appealing to him, but the look of savage anger on his face stopped her from saying anything else.

One black brow lifted patronizingly. ''Why all this sudden show of emotion? A year ago you left me without a backward glance.''

Drawing on her dignity, she whispered, ''Of course I would never stand in your way.''

His mouth thinned into a taut line. "Then I'll bring the papers out to you." He started for the villa.

"Wait—"

Andreas turned back toward her. "What now?" he demanded in a fiery tone.

"I'll sign them, but I was hoping we could talk a little first."

"Isn't that what we've been doing?" His callousness seared her like a blast of fire.

"Please, Andreas—I came all this way to see you."

"Under the circumstances, one phone call would have sufficed."

His dismissive attitude shattered her, but she stood her ground. "Not when it's something as important as our marriage."

"Important?" he mocked. "You dare use that word with me when you've spent a precious year we can't get back demanding I give you a divorce?"

"I know what I've done, but there were reasons. If you'd just hear me out, I would like—"

"What is it you really want?" he cut her off brutally.

This was it.

She smoothed the hair away from her temples. "I'd like us to live together for a month to see if we can find our way back to each other again."

There was a long, sustained silence while he stared at her as if he couldn't believe what he'd just heard. His black gaze probed every square inch of her flushed face and body until she quivered.

"Obviously the idea is abhorrent to you," she murmured in an aching voice.

He swore softly, but that only made her more determined.

"I don't think thirty days out of a whole lifetime is too much to ask. If things don't work out, we'll have the rest of our lives to go our separate ways."

"Not if I make you pregnant." He fired his answer back so fast, she was incredulous. "Are you afraid your cancer will come back before you can have a baby? Is that what this is all about? One more month to try to become a mother?"

"Andreas—" She let out an agonized cry. "Of course not!"

His sudden intake of breath sounded like ripping silk.

"Even if that was what I wanted, I have no idea if I'm fertile. A twenty-five pound weight gain doesn't necessarily ensure results—not after my bout with cancer."

He raked a hand through his black hair, disheveling it. "The trust is gone on both sides, Dominique."

Her eyes stung with unshed tears. "That's why I want to try again. We could pretend we have no history and it's the first time for both of us."

"You mean wash the slate clean?" he insinuated, with a raw cynicism that tore up her insides.

"Yes."

"That's not possible."

She raised her chin defiantly. "I admit it would be a challenge, but I've never known you to back down from one."

There was an ominous gleam in his eyes. "When the water got too rough you ran away from our marriage," he accused. "It'll get rough again."

"You're talking about Olympia?"

The shutters flew down across his face. He didn't bother to deny it. Another devastating blow. But she refused to let him know how deeply the knowledge affected her.

"I've always been aware of your feelings for her, and hers for you. She's a permanent fixture in your life. The only thing I require is that you stay out of her bed for the next thirty days to see if we can rekindle the spark. But if that's asking too much, then tell me now. I can't clap with only one hand."

"Neither can I."

The implication jolted her. "What do you mean?"

"In case you've forgotten, we had other issues during our brief marriage," he informed her gravely. "I'm in the middle of some important negotiations that mean I have to do a lot of entertaining in Athens this month."

"In other words I would be an embarrassment to you, like I was before."

"Did I ever say that?"

"You didn't have to. Your late nights at the office, your long silences—they did it for you."

Andreas shot her a withering glance. "As I recall, you didn't like living in Athens and preferred to stay on Zakynthos, out of sight, which made it more difficult for us to be together."

"That's true. I didn't want to be in the city, where I had to share my husband with a lot of other people. I was too madly in love to remember that you had an empire to run and money to earn in order to keep my fantasy alive. It was naïve of me, I know. The truth is, our honeymoon was so wonderful, I hoped it would go on forever.''

"You think I didn't?'' he thundered emotionally.

That was the question Dominique had come back to Greece to ask. She took a fortifying breath.

"You married a blushing, young, needy bride who selfishly thought only of her own pleasure. In that regard I'm afraid I followed the path of most twenty-two-year-old newlyweds.''

His features hardened. "And now you're at the ripe old age of twenty-three, which is entirely different?''

The angry sarcasm pouring out of him would destroy her if she let it.

"That's for both of us to find out…if you're willing. Do you need twenty-four hours to think about it?''

A strange smile broke out on his lips, totally at odds with the glacial look in his eyes. "Giving yourself a loophole already?''

With that question she realized she hadn't made a dent in his armor. The damage had been too great. A year ago she'd left him to face his accuser alone. No doubt the media had pounced all over him like wolves, tearing him to pieces.

"I don't need one. Otherwise I would never have left Sarajevo to come and find you.''

Dominique got to her feet, gazing boldly at him.

"You've asked for a divorce. I'll give it to you. Please tell your pilot to be here first thing in the morning. After I sign the papers, you have my promise I'll be out of your life forever.''

She felt his searching eyes on her bikini-clad body as she left the patio. Instead of darting away, as she would have done once, she walked with confidence, her shoulders back, secretly glad he was drinking his fill of her.

At least when he sent her on her way tomorrow she'd have the satisfaction of knowing it was this image that would stay in his mind.

She'd made it as far as the door of the blue bedroom when she heard him say, "You've gone to the wrong room."

Dominique hadn't realized he'd followed her from the pool. She swung around in complete surprise.

He stared at her through hooded eyes. "The master bedroom is at the other end of the hall."

The breath left her body with a whoosh.

Unbelievably, he'd just announced that their thirty-day trial was going to start tonight.

Her heart hammered so hard she feared it would resonate off the walls. Forcing herself to maintain an outward calm, she said, "I'll get my things from the guest bedroom."

Andreas gave her an almost imperceptible nod. "While you do that I have some phone calls to make before joining you."

"I'll see you in a few minutes, then," she said in a husky voice.

"Dominique—?"

Just the way he said her name, in that vibrant male voice, made her tremble. "Yes?"

He eyed her with brooding intensity. "I'm warning you—I don't give us more than a day before everything falls apart."

The former insecure Dominique would have risen to the bait right then, proving his point.

"To be honest, Andreas, I thought you would have thrown me off the island by now."

She watched his teeth grind together as he disappeared to the other part of the villa.

The only reason he'd agreed to her request was because he was convinced it was too late for them. In his mind he wouldn't have to put up with her much longer.

But for Dominique his capitulation had moved the first giant impediment from her path. Gratified by this much progress, she rushed around the bedroom to gather up her things, euphoric he'd agreed to the temporary arrangement, yet terrified it might all blow up in her face tomorrow, just as he'd prophesied.

But she wasn't too terrified to be feverish with excitement for the night ahead. Without wasting any time, she hurried down the hall to the spacious white master bedroom, with its splashes of yellow, blue and red color. She particularly loved the arched windows that looked out over the ocean.

It had been a long time since she'd walked across these tiles and inhaled the scent of jasmine coming from outside while she anticipated hours of ecstasy in his strong arms.

Before she did anything else she headed for the shower in the *en suite* bathroom to wash her hair. After she'd given it a good lather, and rinsed off, she opted for a towel rather than the blowdryer. Once she'd brushed the gleaming strands into a semblance of order, she entered the bedroom.

Many nights in this room she'd known her husband's possession, but this night was going to be different from all the others.

She reached for her purse. Inside was her diamond wedding ring. She put it on her ring finger, not having worn it since she'd left Greece. All this time she'd felt naked without it.

Purposely leaving a lamp on, she slid beneath the covers without the benefit of a nightgown. In the whole of their marriage she'd never gone to bed without wearing modest nightwear, cut high around the neck. For that matter she'd never worn a bathing suit without a T-shirt.

She'd always insisted that the lights be turned off. If he couldn't see the scar, then she couldn't see it in her mind's eye either. Under the cover of darkness she could pretend she was desirable to her husband.

Andreas had always been understanding and tender with her. He'd never forced her to do anything that made her uncomfortable. But on their wedding night, when his lips had kissed her scar, she had asked him never to do it again. He'd respected her wishes.

Before the wedding Olympia had related what Theo had supposedly told her, that he found Andreas very courageous for marrying Dominique. The implication being that she was a woman whose thin body didn't have all its parts, thereby detracting from the age-old ritual.

After her meeting with Theo today she knew Olympia had lied, and understood the reasons why. But a year ago that remark had wormed its way into Dominique's troubled psyche. It had destroyed her underpinnings to the degree that she'd never taken the initiative in making love with Andreas. He'd always been the one to turn to her. He'd been the one who did all the talking.

That way Dominique had been able to convince herself that when he reached for her it was because he wanted her. Later, when he'd fallen asleep, she would lie there in the dark with hot, silent tears trickling onto her pillow, fearing he'd made love to her out of pity.

When she'd left Andreas, it had taken months of psychiatric therapy in New York for Dominique to understand her feelings of inadequacy, to comprehend why she'd run away from her husband. Through those tough sessions she'd learned why she'd bought into Olympia's and anyone else's comments, which at times could have been construed as insensitive, even cruel.

Once she'd faced her demons, Dominique had undergone a dramatic emotional healing, allowing her to make choices that were right for her.

One of them had been to treat herself as the attractive woman she'd been before she'd ever been diagnosed with cancer, rather than resign herself to being a withered shadow of her former self.

Another choice had been reconstructive surgery, a decision that had indicated she was in good mental health, in charge of own happiness, because no one else could choose that for her but herself.

Understanding that principle had made her free. She no longer feared being cut and probed again. It was a necessary step in the process of achieving total emotional and psychological recovery. The result was that, whether she and Andreas ended up together or not, now she felt whole and feminine.

If her cancer came back, and she had to have the other breast removed, so be it. Never again would she allow herself, events, or other people, to sabotage her self-image.

For the first time in their lives she was unafraid to be with Andreas. No more inhibitions. She was eager to meet him head on, whether it be in love, war, or everything else in between.

A vital issue was at stake here. If he'd been unfaithful to her in his heart, then she needed to hear those words from his lips before she decided on her next course of action.

But first she had to find a way to regain his trust so he would confide in her. Until that happened, their marriage didn't have a prayer of making it.

She turned on her side as if she were facing Andreas, and waited for him to come to her.

CHAPTER FOUR

ANDREAS finished doing laps in the pool before he levered himself to the patio and phoned Olympia.

"I've been waiting to hear from you. Did you catch up with Dominique?"

As concerned and understanding as Olympia had always been, he didn't like discussing Dominique with her.

"Yes."

"I assume you worked everything out and she's on her way back to Bosnia?"

Your assumption's wrong.

All their theories of Dominique wanting money had to be tossed because of Dominique's request. It had blown him away.

Before he joined his estranged wife in the bed she hadn't slept in for more months than he cared to remember, Andreas had needed a workout in the pool to get his head on straight.

He sleeked back his wet hair. "Olympia—"

"When you say my name that way, I know something's wrong. What is it?"

"I won't be able to spend any time with you and Ari for a while. But the yacht is yours to enjoy for as long as you wish. Feel free to come to the villa on Zakynthos. Check with Paul if you need anything."

"That's very generous of you, Andreas. I assume a

business problem has come up you have to deal with?''

''No. This is personal.''

''I see. How long do you think it will be before we can spend some time together, then?''

''I'm not sure. Possibly next month.''

''Next month? What's happened?''

Dominique had come back into his life. That was what had happened.

''I'm going to try to salvage my marriage.''

After a pregnant pause, ''Is she ill again? Needing your support?''

His brows furrowed in irritation. ''If she is, I'll deal with it.''

''I hate to think of you getting hurt a second time.''

He grimaced. ''Let me worry about that.''

''Ari's going to miss you.''

''I'll make time to see him. Goodnight, Olympia.''

He pulled on his trousers before gathering the rest of his clothes to walk through the house to the bedroom.

Nothing could have astonished him more than to discover Dominique lying in bed wide awake with the side lamp turned on. From what he could tell, she wasn't wearing anything but the covers and the wedding ring he'd given her.

His heart did a swift kick.

''I was afraid you weren't coming.'' Her voice sounded husky.

That comment was another first for her. Never once in their marriage had she admitted that she looked forward to going to bed with him, not even with her eyes.

Only under the shield of darkness could he coax her into his arms.

Tonight everything was different.

Those deep set orbs watching him glinted purple in the light. Combined with her sculptured mouth, the flush on her white skin and her silvery-blond hair fanned out on the pillow, he'd never seen a more beautiful woman.

It crucified him to think cancer might ever ravage her again.

"I won't be long," he said, before heading for the bathroom.

The sight of her had left his body trembling. His legs felt heavy as he stepped into the stall. He was scarcely aware of his physical surroundings. Maybe he was having a fantastic dream.

Afraid he would wake up from a dream and find himself alone, he finished his shower in record time. Though his hair was still moist after a brief toweling, he threw on a robe and emerged from the bathroom holding his breath.

When he saw she was still there, with a tantalizing smile curving her mouth, his lungs expelled the air trapped there. He saw no hesitation in her expression, only a radiant eagerness.

If it was a façade to prove she'd changed, it was a damn good one. Andreas discovered for the first time in his life he was nervous.

Anyone would think *he* was the feverish bride, anticipating the first night in her lover's arms.

"No— Don't—" she urged softly when he reached for the lamp switch. "I want to see you."

Her words checked his movements, almost giving him a heart attack.

"When I woke up after my accident and saw you staring down at me, I thought you were the most beautiful man I'd ever laid eyes on."

Andreas's throat thickened.

"I didn't know there was a man born who could look like you. I deliberately tried to keep from staring at you. Even after we were married I was afraid to look too long because I didn't want you to think I was…begging you."

"Begging me?" he whispered incredulously. "To do what?"

"To make love to me."

He shook his dark head. "If I needed to be begged, I would never have proposed to you."

Her lower lip trembled. "I—I wanted to believe that. But every time I looked at myself in the mirror, I wanted to die, because I could never be the fulfillment of any man's dreams—let alone my husband's."

Dumbstruck, Andreas sank down at the side of the bed. "Then how do you explain my attraction to you?"

She stared up into his eyes, searching them. "There's a basic kindness in you, Andreas. It runs very deep. You saw the accident that knocked me unconscious, a-and you saw my scar. I know how you honor valor, and realized you viewed me as some kind of heroine because I'd had a battle with cancer."

He took a fierce breath. "So from that you deduced I felt so sorry for all you'd been through I asked you to be my wife?"

Her head moved from side to side on the pillow.

"Not just that. I knew you were still mourning Maris's death. The two of you were close all your lives. Your parents' lives were shattered. I think your feelings of helplessness and despair had a lot to do with your reaching out to me. Like one of those dying children who's granted their greatest wish. I believed you saw me as someone needing help."

He swore under his breath.

"Earlier today Theo told me that when he first met me I reminded him of a fledgling bird who required protection."

Theo be damned.

Andreas shot to his feet and started pacing. He couldn't believe what he was hearing. "If that's the way you perceived things, it's a miracle our marriage lasted as long as it did."

"I agree," she murmured. "It's one thing I've learned this past year. Even if it was the wrong perception, it was my reality at the time."

His feet came to a standstill. "So what are you saying?"

She exhaled a tortured sigh. "I'm on a mission to discover the true reality of our lives. It means starting over from scratch, but I'm willing to do anything to make our marriage work, provided you are too.

"Please don't get me wrong," she cried before he could respond. "Before you tell me again that it's pointless, let me admit up front that I'm the one to blame for our problems. When you tried to get me to open up, I froze. It's no wonder you had to walk on eggshells around me. You're a man with infinite patience. I took advantage of that remarkable trait and continued to behave like a spoiled, difficult child. The nicer and kinder you were to me, the worse I acted. You have no idea how I loathed myself." Her voice shook.

"When you told me Theo had charged you with adultery, deep down inside I wanted to tell him it was my fault, that if he wanted revenge he should have come after me. I was the real culprit. Instead, I ran away like the coward I was. But I've had a year of psychiatric therapy to understand myself, and—"

"Therapy?"

"Yes. Don't tell me that shocks you—not when we both know how badly I needed it."

"I'm not shocked." His voice grated.

She bit her lip. "Surprised, then."

"If anything I'm amazed you would put yourself through that experience, considering you've had more surgery too." Twelve months she'd deprived him of being there for her.

"Without the therapy I would never have decided to go in for reconstructive surgery. I think the doctor did a wonderful job. She told me only my husband would know for sure."

Her humor awed him.

Her courage moved him to tears.

"Dominique—"

"I do believe my husband is speechless. I wonder if that's good or bad." She flashed him an impish smile, producing the dimple in her left cheek he hadn't seen for a year.

"Come to bed." She raised her soft, graceful arms toward him. "I've been waiting for this a long, long time."

His heart was palpitating right out of his chest.

Slowly he removed his robe and slid on the mattress beside the siren who by some miracle was still his wife. "I want to look at you first."

She wound her arms around his neck, then brushed her lips teasingly against his. "We have a year to catch up on. It may take the whole night."

There'd always been passion in their lovemaking. But she'd never met him as an equal before. Not like this.

Andreas pulled her on top of him and chased her mouth until he caught it. Exciting laughter gurgled from her throat before they looked without fear or striving into each other's eyes. Then they began moving and breathing as one.

Dominique awakened at dawn with a sense of well-being she'd never known in her life. Her arms automatically reached for the man who'd brought her ecstasy last night. When she couldn't find him, she sat up and smoothed strands of hair from her face.

Over at the window, facing the ocean, she detected his tall, distinctive silhouette. In the faint light she barely discerned the outline of his striped robe.

Moving off the bed, she found one of the T-shirts from his drawer and drew it over her head. It fell to mid-thigh.

Quietly she padded across the room and slid her arms around his waist from behind. "Good morning," she whispered, standing on tiptoe to kiss his nape where the black curls swirled. She adored his hair, which was thick and luxuriant. She adored him.

"Mmm. You smell so good," she murmured, squeezing him hard. "You have your own male scent. If I could market it, I would call it 'Strictly Andreas.'"

She didn't know what she'd expected by way of response, but not the solemn-faced man who turned to her.

He kissed both her palms before letting her go. "I'm sorry if I wakened you."

The most important thing she'd learned in therapy was to get everything out in the open as soon as possible so there'd be no chance for misunderstandings to fester.

"You didn't. I woke up on my own, eager to take my husband into my arms, but you weren't there. Obviously something's on your mind. Let's talk about it."

"Not right now."

"Yes," she insisted. "Right now."

Lines darkened his face.

"This is how things started to go wrong for us the first time, Andreas. I'd hide and avoid…cut and run. You would hold back, go quiet, retreat. We can't do that anymore. Tell me what's troubling you, even if you're afraid it will cause problems."

It was growing lighter outside. She could see the tautness around his mouth, the shadows under his eyes that hadn't been there during the night.

"You told me you'd seen the doctor right before you came to Greece."

"That's true."

The tension emanating from him was fierce. "I take it you were referring to Dr. Canfield, the plastic surgeon?"

"Yes. She gave me a clean bill of health."

He rubbed the back of his neck in a gesture that always signaled frustration. "What about your cancer specialist?"

"I saw Dr. Josephson too. So far I'm cancer-free."

His eyes narrowed on her mouth. "You wouldn't lie to me—"

Apparently the change in her had unearthed some demons he'd kept well hidden until now.

"Why would I do that? What purpose would it serve? As you know, I have to be tested once a month. From now on we'll go to the doctor together and hear the results at the same time."

Andreas took a shuddering breath. "Did Dr. Josephson suggest you have another mastectomy as a preventative measure?"

"No—" She shook her head in bewilderment. "He doesn't think it's necessary in my case."

Andreas pursed his lips. "Maybe you should get a second opinion."

"Then we will," she said, wanting to appease him in any way she could. But by the anxious expression on his face her husband still wasn't reassured.

"What else are you worried about?" If she wasn't mistaken, he'd paled.

"Before our separation, I always took precautions."

"True… So what happened last night?"

His hands suddenly grasped her shoulders. "You know what happened," he groaned in self-abnegation. "I lost my head."

"Imagine Andreas Stamatakis of all men doing something as wild and irresponsible as that—" She grinned up at him. "I think I'm going to take it as the most supreme compliment of my life that I had that kind of power over you last night."

He gave her a shake, not realizing his strength. "This isn't a joking matter, Dominique. What if I've made you pregnant?"

She sobered. "If you're convinced our marriage isn't going to last, then I understand your concern."

"That's not the point and you know it," he muttered grimly. "I'm concerned about your health."

"We had this conversation before we got married. Dr. Josephson said there was no reason why we couldn't try for a baby. Cancer only affects about one in a thousand pregnancies."

His fingers tightened on her warm skin. "I remember the statistics, but it's you we're talking about."

"If you're suggesting I take a 'morning after' pill, then I guess our marriage really is over, because I would never, ever harm my baby."

His hands ran the length of her arms with restless urgency. "It might be the only option if it meant your life was in danger."

Dominique had never known him to be afraid of anything, but it was raw fear she could hear in his voice.

When she'd asked him for thirty days to see if they could save their marriage, she never dreamed a destructive emotion like fear would head the list of obstacles he would have to overcome.

"I'm not going to die for a long time, Andreas. Last year the doctor's main concern was that I was underweight. It can make conception more difficult. Right now I'm in perfect shape and I refuse to look for trouble when there isn't any. But that's only my perception, of course. You mentioned other issues we have to work through.''

Nothing she said seemed to make any difference. Talking only proved to increase his tension. The situation required some serious action.

''I've forgotten this *is* only day two of our temporary reconciliation,'' she said with a little smile. ''According to your calculations, everything's supposed to fall apart today. If that's the case, why don't we go back to bed and make the most of the hours we have left?''

''Be serious,'' he whispered in a tortured breath.

''I'm being very serious,'' she claimed with mock severity. Backing away from him, she got under the covers to remove her T-shirt. Then she wadded it up and threw it at him.

It hit him smack in the chest.

His sudden bark of laughter was the most gratifying sound she'd heard in a long time. Before the next beat of her heart he'd reached her, and had pinned her back against the pillows. Their mouths were only a centimeter apart.

She gazed with daring into his fiery black eyes. ''You move fast for an old man. Do you know that?''

''Old?'' he growled. ''I'll show you old.''

Three hours later, Dominique surfaced first. Carefully she untangled herself from the strong arms and legs twined around her. Andreas had made love to her with primitive need. Now his Greek god-like body needed sleep.

Though she was still on fire for her exhausted husband, she disciplined herself not to waken him.

Hopefully the American breakfast she planned to serve him in bed would bring him back to her.

He rarely ate breakfast. Just coffee, sometimes a roll. He made up for it at his other meals. But not today.

After a quick shower, she put on a sundress, then fastened her hair in a ponytail. As she darted through the villa to the kitchen Eleni caught up to her.

"You need something?"

Dominique shook her head. "No, thank you. I'm going to fix us some breakfast."

"I'll call Anna."

"That's all right. I want to do this for my husband."

"You're sure?"

Clearly Eleni didn't know what to make of the situation. Andreas's staff had always waited on him. It was Dominique's fault she'd never asserted herself or interfered with the routine. But all that was about to change, starting now.

"Would you be kind enough to show me where everything is? I want to make him a big meal. He's lost weight, don't you think?"

To her relief, the other woman nodded with a smile. "It's good for him you've come back."

Ah, Eleni...I needed to hear that.

They worked together like two conspirators. And before long she carried a tray to the master suite. To her delight, Andreas's eyes opened when she approached the bed.

"I come bearing gifts. Sit up and I shall serve you, my lord."

His white smile was more dazzling because of the

shadow from his beard. After he'd done her bidding, she set the tray across his lap.

"I didn't know Anna could cook food like this—"

"Not Anna—me!"

His surprised gaze swerved to her face.

"Don't worry. I cleared it with Eleni, so no one's feelings would be hurt."

She puffed up a couple of pillows next to him, then climbed on the bed and reached for her own plate. After tucking in, it thrilled her to watch him devour his pile of French toast and scrambled eggs with equal relish. He drank his orange juice never once stopping for breath.

"How odd," she remarked while she sipped her juice. "Eleni was under the impression you didn't have a big appetite anymore. I have to say I don't see anything wrong with it. In fact for an old man you've surprised me in quite a few ways I wasn't expecting."

He cast her a sidelong glance. "For a child bride you've managed to pull off several surprises yourself."

"Maybe we should take you to the doctor and get your heart checked out. Just in case."

"You little minx."

Suddenly everything was thrust away. She let out a yelp of laughter as he rolled her up in his arms. They were both out of breath.

"Thank you for breakfast. It was almost as delicious as you are."

The corner of her mouth curved upward. "You think I'm delicious?"

His low chuckle drove her mad with excitement.

"How do you say that in Greek?"

"Ask me later," he murmured against her lips. "Right now I have more important things to do."

"Careful of the tray!"

Her warning came too late. The sound of plates and glasses crashing on the tiles made her wince.

"No—" she cried, holding him down. "I've got sandals on. One step and you could cut yourself."

"Leave it!" he demanded, preventing her from sliding off the bed. "The staff will take care of it."

"They shouldn't have to deal with something that's our fault."

"It's what I pay them for."

"To do regular work, yes—"

"The occasional accident *is* regular work to them."

They'd had this argument before.

"I'm sorry." She molded her palms to his cheeks. "I didn't grow up with staff around. My first instinct is to do everything myself." She studied his gleaming black eyes. "I love doing things for you, but not if it means upsetting you and your world."

His chest rose and fell visibly. "Let's get something straight. I like my wife looking after me. When we're—"

The ringing of the house phone prevented him from finishing what he was about to say.

"That's probably Eleni. She wouldn't disturb us if it weren't important." Still holding Dominique close, he reached for the receiver by the lamp to speak to his housekeeper.

The conversation was brief. His dark brows knit together. She knew something was wrong.

*   *   *

Andreas hadn't anticipated his reunion with Dominique would sweep him away to a place where he wanted to stay with her forever, far from everyone and everything. She'd brought him ecstasy on a brand new level. He felt reborn.

But, as miraculous as the last twelve hours had been, he wasn't so blind that he didn't know their marriage was still in a fragile state. There was so much that needed sorting out—problems they hadn't even touched on yet.

When he'd warned her things would probably start to fall apart between them within a twenty-four-hour period, he hadn't realized how accurate his prediction would be.

With one phone call reality had intruded, to tear at the fabric of their newfound joy much sooner than he'd suspected.

The pain of last year's separation would be nothing compared to the agony he would suffer if their trial reconciliation foundered in deep waters, never to be resurrected again.

"We have visitors," he stated grimly, after hanging up the phone.

"Who?"

"Paul's helping Olympia get settled in with Ari. It's her vacation. Since I have to be back in Athens, I told her she was free to use the yacht and the villa."

He watched her violet eyes, waiting to see them cloud now that she'd heard the news. Amazingly, they stayed clear.

"Like I told you earlier, you're the kindest, most generous man I've ever known. Hurry and shower while I help her with Ari. But please get out on *my* side of the bed, darling. I don't want to have to rush you to the doctor for your heart *and* cut feet.''

She gave him a long, passionate kiss before disappearing from their bedroom. Dazed by her response, Andreas could only stare after her. His wife had changed so much.

CHAPTER FIVE

THROUGH the windows at the east side of the villa Dominique could see Paul bringing a load of things from the helicopter. She rushed outside.

"Hi, Paul! What can I do to help?"

He gaze roved over her features, settling on her ponytail. Obviously her new look kept surprising him. "This is the last of it."

"Let me take that thing under your arm." She grabbed the clear plastic holder. It contained what looked like a colorful little quilted floor gym.

"Thank you."

"You're welcome."

Eleni met them at the entrance. "I've put Olympia in the pink room. She's warming a bottle for the little one in the kitchen."

"Perfect. Come on, Paul. Let's set up the crib for Ari."

"I've already done it."

"You're a wonder, you know that?"

A rare smile broke out on his face. It made him quite good-looking. According to Andreas, he'd had various relationships with women over the years, but none of them had ever lasted.

He followed her down the hall to the bedroom. Ari was lying in his crib, contemplating his toes, but one glimpse of Dominique and his cute little face crumpled.

"I have a terrible effect on him," she lamented to Paul as the baby started to wail. "The other day the same thing happened."

"He doesn't know you. Come on, Ari." He said something else in Greek and plucked the baby from the mattress. Immediately the little guy stopped crying, but he still stared at Dominique as if she were the enemy.

"Well, Uncle Paul..." She delighted in teasing him. "Who would have guessed you have the master touch?"

"Paul's full of hidden talents."

Dominique swung around to confront her husband, who was freshly shaven. He'd donned white slacks, and a navy polo shirt covered his well-defined chest. Just looking at his virile face and body drove the air from her lungs.

When her gaze switched to Paul, she caught him blushing.

How could it be that for all the time she'd known Andreas's friend, a man who'd always seemed rather formidable, she hadn't understood he was really shy and sweet? The year away had given her second sight about a lot of things.

"I want to check this out." She opened the little gym and placed it on the tile floor. Padded toys dangled from an arc.

"Paul? Let's see what Ari does with it."

"He loves this."

The minute he set him down, the baby started kicking at the various animals with all his might. He really did love it. While he lay there, Dominique picked out the features that were Olympia's. His body shape and hairline reminded her of Theo.

A pain pierced her heart to think Theo had cut himself off from his own flesh and blood. Every child deserved its father if it was at all possible.

Dominique adored her dad. He'd always been so wonderful to her, but never more than when she'd cried to him on the phone after finding out she had cancer. When he'd told her she was going to be all right, it had been as if God had been speaking to her.

Little Ari would never know what that was like.

Her eyes smarted for him and Theo.

Suddenly she felt Andreas's gaze trained on her and glanced over at him. For a second she thought she saw pain.

Was he still worrying that he might have gotten her pregnant?

In therapy she'd learned about the loved ones of cancer victims. They suffered in their own way too, and had to work through their grief.

Dominique could see she'd done a lot of damage in the past by not letting Andreas talk about it and share it with her. He'd had to shut off in order to placate her. Now he didn't know where to go with all his feelings.

Later, when they were alone, she would force him to tell her everything he was thinking and obsessing about, even if the conversation became repetitive. An open dialogue was the only way to help him cope with the future.

Her attention returned to Ari. Unable to help it, she knelt down to tickle his little tummy. "You cute little thing. You're adorable."

He stared at her with large, startled brown eyes.

"Ari doesn't know what to make of me."

"My son's not used to hearing English." His mother spoke from the doorway.

Dominique got to her feet. "He's a beautiful boy, Olympia. You're so lucky to have him."

"I think so too."

"It looks like you're ready to feed him, so we'll leave you alone."

"Do you want to give him his bottle?"

Olympia's demeanor had undergone a change from two days ago. What was going on?

"I'm afraid there isn't time," Andreas answered before Dominique could say anything. "The pilot's waiting to fly us to Athens. I've already arranged for your things to be put on board, Dominique."

They were leaving for Athens right this minute?

She couldn't believe it, but now was not the time to question her husband's decision.

Turning to Olympia, she said, "There's nothing I'd love more than to feed your baby. When you're back in Athens, please bring him to the penthouse so he can get to know me better. Then maybe he won't cry when I try to hold him."

"After my vacation's over, I'll call you."

"I'd like that very much."

Dominique was more than ready to play Olympia's game. She reasoned that if they played long and hard enough Olympia would get tired of it and become resigned to the fact that Dominique was here to stay.

She turned to Paul. "Are you coming with Andreas and me?"

"Yes."

He picked up the baby and handed him to Olympia.

"Is there anything else we can do for you before we leave?" Andreas inquired.

Olympia shook her head. "You've done too much already. Thank you."

He kissed the top of the baby's head. When he raised up, his gaze flew to Dominique's. "Shall we go?"

"Just let me get my purse."

She hurried to the master bedroom, then popped in the bathroom to remove the elastic holding up her hair and gave it a brush. Now she felt ready to leave.

After racing through the villa to the chopper, Andreas helped her climb on board. He took his place in the co-pilot's seat. Paul sat across from her. Once they were strapped in, the pilot made a flawless ascent and headed for Athens.

To her chagrin Andreas wore a brooding expression once more. The thrilling lover of last night was nowhere to be found. With second sight she realized he was hiding his feelings and confusion behind that remote mask.

Not to be put off, Dominique turned to Paul and forced him to talk about his childhood with Andreas. He rewarded her by relating some of their more notorious escapades. She laughed out loud so hard he and the pilot laughed too. It made their short trip very enjoyable.

A company limo was waiting for them at the airport. They dropped Paul off at his flat, then continued on to Andreas's penthouse apartment, with its elegant, cosmopolitan furnishings and a view of the Acropolis to die for.

She looked out over the city. Nothing seemed changed from a year ago. But as she heard Andreas bringing in their things she was assailed by bittersweet memories. The last time she'd been in here was the morning they'd gotten ready to leave for the courthouse. The beginning of the end for her.

At that point in time she'd felt deserted by his parents, who'd never shown her much warmth and had closed ranks to protect their son no matter what. Her four-month-old marriage had been hanging by a thread. The tension between her and Andreas had made it impossible to communicate. Every look wounded. Every gesture was misinterpreted.

Dominique hadn't known what to believe about him and Olympia. Andreas had asked her to trust him. But it hadn't seemed possible to her that Theo would charge them as adulterers for the whole world to see…unless it were true.

For Theo to do something so awful had shaken her faith in her marriage, in Andreas. It had made a lie of any friendship she'd tried to cultivate with Olympia. Nothing had made sense.

She hadn't been able to follow much of the Greek spoken at the opening of the trial, but she'd known the essence of it. Suddenly the walls had seemed to close in. Everyone's wooden faces, the clamoring of the media outside in the halls—it had all been too much and it had suffocated her.

Paul must have been watching her, because he'd followed her outside to the limo amidst a barrage of photographers and camera flashes flanking them.

Looking back on that day, she recalled Paul's desperate attempt to get her to reconsider. He'd ridden all the way to the airport with her, begging her not to leave Andreas. But she'd been beyond reach.

Thinking about it now, she realized how much Paul loved Andreas. He had tried to stop her. That alone should have told her there was more to the story than she knew. Maybe deep down she *had* known, but her own doubts about her validity as a woman had blinded her to certain truths.

"Dominique?" She turned to her husband. There was a whiteness around his mouth. He looked ill. "I want you to get Dr. Josephson on the phone."

She'd been right. He was fixated on the fact that they'd made love without protection.

"His numbers are in my purse." She walked over to the glass coffee table and pulled a small address book from her wallet. "It's morning in New York. He could still be home, but he might be making rounds at the hospital before he goes to the office. I'll try to find him."

Andreas handed her his cellphone. She sat down on the couch and placed a call to the doctor's office first. The receptionist said she was expecting him shortly and he would phone Dominique as soon as he came in.

She clicked off, then darted him a glance. "He's on his way to work and will call us."

Anxious to alleviate his anxiety, she got up and walked over to him. Grasping his hands, she said, "Would it help if I tell you it's not time for me to be ovulating yet? If I'd thought there was any chance for me to conceive, I would have talked to you about it first."

She felt his body shudder with relief.

"Don't misunderstand me, Andreas. I want a baby. Your baby. But I asked you if we could have this trial period to see if we could make a real marriage between us. Until we know it's rock-solid, we have no business bringing a child into the world."

His hands slid to her shoulders. "I couldn't agree more. Last night I wasn't think—"

The rest of the words came out muffled because she'd covered his lips with hers to quiet them. "Last night was the most glorious night of my life. That's the way it should be when two people are in love. Please don't ruin it with regrets."

"Dominique—"

He crushed her mouth with his own, sweeping them away to the same place they'd gone last night. Yet the way he clung to her revealed needs and fears he hadn't yet articulated.

There was so much she still had to understand about her husband. God willing, they would make it through the next month and have a stronger union for it.

Just as he'd picked her up and started for the bedroom his cellphone rang. "That's probably Dr. Josephson," she said when he relinquished her mouth.

He carried her over to the couch and sat down with her on his lap. She reached for the phone and identified herself. It was the doctor.

"Hello, Dominique. My receptionist said you were anxious to talk to me. What's going on?"

"Actually, it's my husband who would like some questions answered. Do you have time now?"

"Is he right there?"

"Yes."

"Put him on."

Their conversation went on long enough that she slid off his lap and went into the kitchen for drinks. He kept a stock of juices in the fridge. She pulled two from the rack and carried them back to the living room.

Whatever Dr. Josephson said must have relieved her husband somewhat. When he hung up, more animation lit his handsome features. His black eyes didn't appear as haunted.

She removed the cap and handed him a bottle of ice-cold lemonade. He took it and devoured most of the contents before setting it down on the table.

"That tasted good," he murmured, studying her intently.

"I thought we could both use one."

His intimate gaze traveled down her figure. "I like your dress. The colors blend perfectly with your hair and skin."

Her body started to tremble. "It's simple."

"It's stunning."

"Thank you."

"Paul told me you came to Greece without luggage."

"I bought a few items in Fiskardo."

"Enough for all of two days," he said dryly.

She had an idea where this conversation was leading. It was on the tip of her tongue to tell him she would ask her parents to ship her wardrobe from Sarajevo. But at the last second she caught herself.

In the past she'd never let Andreas go shopping for clothes with her. She'd returned the one outfit he'd bought for her without trying it on. It had been a dress a little like the one she was wearing, but she'd wanted something that hugged her neck and hid her body. She hadn't felt beautiful, and had preferred that her thin arms were covered too.

Andreas was a generous man who liked to give pleasure to everyone. But she'd deprived him of bestowing little surprises on her. Sometimes, like now, she wondered how he'd put up with her as long as he did.

"Do you have to stop in at the office this afternoon?"

"No."

"Then let's go shopping in Kolonaki." It was a trendy residential neighborhood in the center of Athens, full of pricey boutiques, art galleries and expensive restaurants. The kind of place she knew he'd yearned to take her.

His eyes ignited. "We'll have a meal there too."

"First I'll want you to choose some outfits that will be appropriate for me to wear when we entertain guests this month. If we eat first, I'll need your help to fasten everything."

His wolfish smile proved that she'd said the right thing. After his talk with the doctor, his angst appeared mitigated. At least for the time being.

Two hours later they'd arranged for an entire wardrobe of dresses, separates and shoes to be delivered to the penthouse the next day. She'd never had so much fun.

Sharing everything with her husband was a new experience she intended to keep alive. And that meant developing a relationship with his parents.

Over a fabulous meal of moussaka, she brought them into the conversation. "I know you have a lot of business and entertaining to do this month, but do you think we could squeeze your parents in one night soon for dinner?''

When he went still like that, it meant she'd surprised him. She could hear his mind digesting her idea while he wiped the corner of his mouth with a napkin.

"Friday night's free. I'll call them and arrange it.''

"That would be wonderful. I want to really get to know them. When you introduced us, you told me they were still in so much pain over Maris's death they weren't themselves. But I should have made more of an effort to get us together after our return to Athens. The trouble was, no time seemed the right time.''

"That's because there wasn't one.''

Andreas spoke the truth. The threat of the trial had loomed too large to deal with anything else.

She gazed at him directly. "Do you think they'll come?''

"Of course.''

"Even if they believe I'm a poor excuse for a wife?''

"That's not their opinion of you,'' he declared, in that tone of authority he used on his business calls.

Dominique couldn't help but smile a little sadly. "It's every parent's opinion when anyone hurts their child. I didn't stand by you at the trial. Therefore I failed you, and as a result failed them. I'd like to repair the damage.''

Instinctively Dominique realized their marriage could never be completely happy until she'd been accepted by his mother and father. She had a long way to go, but Friday night could be the first step.

"You're sure you want to do this?" His eyes were shuttered—his way of veiling his torturous emotions.

"More than anything in the world. My parents think the world of you. I'm hoping that one day yours will feel the same about me."

His mouth tautened in response. "If you're telling me the charge of adultery didn't change their feelings, I don't believe you."

She sat forward. "They never passed judgment on you. Not once. You were so marvelous to me after my accident, they've never forgotten and refuse to believe anything bad about you."

After a silence, "I've always admired them too. Very much, in fact."

"Unfortunately your parents' first introduction to me came as a shock. I was a young American girl, the antithesis of the Greek woman they had in mind for their only son. I couldn't say more than a few phrases in your language. I certainly didn't look as if I could produce a grandchild for them."

His features darkened. "Who told you those things?" he demanded harshly.

"No one. Come on, darling. Admit that's exactly how they felt about me."

"You're lying." The words came out more like a breath. "Someone had to put those thoughts in your mind."

Even if someone had, she had no desire to tell him. "I don't need to lie. After looking at the picture of Maris you keep on your desk, I realized it was the truth. If I'd been your mom I would have been disappointed to meet a foreigner like me. Especially one who could have passed for a boy if you didn't look too hard.''

The waiter couldn't have chosen a better time to give them the dessert menus. ''I don't care for any. What about you, Dominique?'' Andreas handed his back without looking at it.

She followed suit. ''The moussaka was so delicious, I couldn't eat another thing right now.''

''Very good.''

As soon as the waiter went away Andreas shot her an angry glance. ''We're not through with this discussion.''

''Andreas—let it go,'' she urged calmly. ''What we've been talking about is long since in the past. All I care about is spending an enjoyable evening with your family. You said you had a lot of old home movies on video packed away somewhere. What would you think if we got them out and showed them? I've always wanted to see them, and I bet your parents would love it too. It might open them up, get them to talk and share some of their feelings. I'd like to think it could bring us all closer together.''

''It's a brilliant idea.''

He meant it or he wouldn't have said it. She was overjoyed, but she wasn't fooled. Andreas would probe until he got that name from her. He'd guessed that someone had influenced her thoughts about his parents. Dominique's only fear was that it would upset him. She'd gotten past her pain ages ago.

After paying the bill, he pushed himself away from the table and came around her side to help her. ''Let's go home and we'll look for them. I think I put some boxes of them on one of the shelves in the guest bedroom.''

They returned to the penthouse in a taxi.

When they entered the foyer, she turned to Andreas. "While you find the boxes, I'll phone my folks. Dad needs to know I'm not coming back to work. We already talked about that eventuality, but I need to make it official.''

"That's something else we need to talk about."

"What?'' she cried, half afraid he was going to tell her their experiment wasn't working after all.

He traced the mold of her facial features with a finger. His touch turned her blood molten.

"I'm not unaware you've held a job during our time apart. Tomorrow I'll get up and go to work, but you'll be here with time on your hands. Much as I wanted a stay-at-home wife, in retrospect I can see that wasn't fair to you.''

Elated by the admission, she said, "You'll always be my first priority, but I do have some plans that won't require punching a time clock. That is if they meet with your approval. After I get off the phone, I'd like to run them past you and get your opinion. I'm expecting you to be totally honest with me.''

"That works both ways,'' he murmured, before heading for the guest bedroom.

Deciding there weren't going to be any more secrets in this house, she followed him. When Andreas discovered she was right behind him, he flashed her a surprised glance. She pressed a kiss to his lips, then sat down on the bed to make her call.

It looked like the closet was a treasure trove of memorabilia he'd collected. She couldn't wait to examine everything, but right now she had a more pressing issue.

"Domani!" Her father always called her that.

"Hi, Dad."

"Your mom's going to have a fit she missed this call. She's over at the Ladislavs' consoling them. Their cat died today."

"Blaz?"

"Yes."

"Oh…I'll send them a sympathy card."

Her father chuckled. "Sounds just like the sort of thing my darling daughter would do. How are you?"

"I'm sitting on a bed at our penthouse, watching my husband clean out a closet I don't think he's touched in years."

Andreas flashed a smile at her over his broad shoulder. She loved his big, gorgeous build. She loved everything about him.

"I take it you won't be coming back to work?"

"No."

"You sound as happy as Blaz looked the other day when I came home from work and saw him with feathers stuck to his whiskers."

"Dad—cats are supposed to eat mice!"

"Evidently he did plenty of that too. It makes you wonder what he's going to chase now that he's gone to heaven."

No one could make her laugh like her father. "I love you."

"We love you too, sweetie. Keep up whatever you're doing, because it sounds like it's working. Don't forget we're rooting for you."

"I know that," she said in a husky tone.

"Give my regards to our favorite son-in-law. When-ever you say the word, we're up for a trip to Athens."

"I'll tell him. Give Mom a kiss for me."

"That won't be a problem."

Her parents were one of the happiest couples she knew. "Goodnight, Dad."

"Stay well, sweetie."

"You too."

She hung up.

By now Andreas had retrieved three boxes which he'd stacked by the door.

"Dad said you were his favorite son-in-law. He asked me to give you his best regards."

Andreas turned to her and pushed her back before following her down onto the bed. "He would have to say that, wouldn't he?" he whispered against her lips.

"No," she answered solemnly. "When I returned to Sarajevo and told them I was divorcing you, they felt like they'd lost a child. Your parents aren't the only people who've been in mourning."

CHAPTER SIX

THE purity of his wife's violet eyes slipped past his defenses to pierce his soul. He twined her silky blond hair in his fingers, loving the texture.

"I want to know the name of the person who put those thoughts about my parents in your head. Views about you they never thought or spoke."

Immediately her expression grew troubled. "It doesn't matter, darling."

"It does to me. Anything that hurts you, hurts me."

"I feel the same way, so let's not crucify ourselves anymore by dredging up the past."

He looked down at her. "If you're covering for Paul, I have to know."

"Andreas—" she cried in genuine alarm. "Of course it's not Paul. He loves you. There isn't anything he wouldn't do for you."

Incredibly relieved, his mind jumped to the only other person he knew who might have taken pleasure in creating trouble in their marriage.

"What kind of power does Theo have over you that you would try to protect him?"

"It wasn't Theo. If I tell you, you might take it the wrong way, so I'd rather not have this discussion."

"Try me."

He felt her shiver. It traveled the length of his body.

"Olympia didn't mean any harm."

Olympia?

"Apparently she and your sister had someone picked out for you long before I came on the scene. A dark-haired beauty from a good Greek family. We laughed about the shock it must have given your parents when you told them you were going to marry me. I agreed with her, and that's all there was to it. Promise me you won't say anything to her. I would be devastated if you did."

He buried his face in her neck, where her scent was the sweetest. "I give you my word."

"Thank you. I'm sure that if your sister were alive she would have said the same thing to me and we would've had a good laugh too. You know that old adage about life happening to you when you have other plans? That premise certainly was true of you and me. If I hadn't discovered the cancer, I would have finished college at NYU. No doubt I would have ended up marrying a New Yorker. And you, my love, would have married someone your family had envisioned for you."

"No one decides my life for me."

"I didn't mean that literally. If I had a brother I'm sure I would see someone and say, 'That's the woman he should marry.' It's human nature. Haven't you ever met a woman you thought might be right for Paul?"

Andreas chuckled. "Touché. You've made your point."

"Good."

Irresistibly drawn to her mouth, he shoved certain disturbing thoughts to the back of his mind and began kissing her. She gave him an electrifying response, unleashing his passion with such overwhelming force he lost all sense of time and place.

Hours later, when they were temporarily sated, she lay wrapped in his arms with her back against his chest. "Darling? Do you realize we've never made love on this bed before?"

There had been so many firsts since she'd come back into his life, he was dizzy from the excitement.

"I know another place we need to christen," he teased, biting her ear.

"So do I, but taking a shower together means getting out of bed. Right now I'm much too content to budge."

His breath caught. "In the morning, then."

"It's a date."

Andreas crushed her against him, so happy he was terrified. "Tell me about these plans that don't require going into an office every day."

She turned so she was facing him. "I'm really excited about it, but you might not feel the same way. So if you have reservations, then I'll propose plan B."

Everything she said and did charmed him to his very core. "Forget B. I want to hear A."

"Spoken like a true Stamatakis." Her eyes shone like purple stars.

"Go on," he urged, kissing the tip of her well-shaped nose.

"It's a given I want to become fluent in Greek, so I'm planning to hire a tutor. Besides that, here's my idea. Prior to my mastectomy, a woman my age, who was a volunteer from the local cancer institute, came to see me—before the operation."

At the mention of her cancer he had to steel himself not to cringe.

"She'd had the same procedure done and explained

her experience. I had so many questions only she
could answer. It was more helpful than you will ever
know. What I'd like to do is gather some other cancer
survivors together under the umbrella of a Stamatakis
Cancer Foundation. It would be a volunteer group that
would eventually visit hospitals and clinics all over
Greece, doing the same job that woman did for me.
Educating me took away a lot of my fear. I'd like to
do that for other women facing the same challenge."

Andreas lay back against the pillow, fighting the
urge to tell her he didn't want to think about her cancer. He wanted it all to go away. But his beautiful,
earnest wife felt so passionately about it he had no
choice but to listen until she was through.

"One of the projects we could do to raise cancer
awareness and save lives is to sponsor a fun run. You
know—the kind of marathon I ran on Zakynthos. But
only cancer survivors would be the ones running. We
could hold them all over Greece. Maybe once every
two or three months. I don't know yet. It would take
a lot of planning, and the cooperation of local government officials, but I think it would be exciting—and
most of all beneficial."

She leaned on his chest and cupped his temples with
her hands. "I know you hate the mere mention of the
word. All loved ones do. But if we face up to it and
fight it together our marriage will be stronger for it.
Naturally this isn't all going to happen overnight. I'll
work on it slowly, around your schedule. But if you'd
rather I didn't do that, then I've been thinking of finishing college here. I don't know how many of my
classes at NYU will transfer, but I do know I want to
get my degree."

A tight band had constricted his breathing. He reached for her hands and kissed the tips of her fingers. "Let me sleep on it."

Her hair brushed against his eyelids. She tucked it around her shell-like ear. "Of course, darling. There's no rush on anything. We have our whole lives ahead of us."

Our whole lives.

She was so brave. He couldn't find the words to tell her.

"Don't put me on some kind of angelic pedestal," she said, reading his mind. "Hundreds of thousands of women around the world are in my exact shoes." She smiled. "There's a whole whacked army of us."

"A formidable army," he admitted in a haunted whisper. "My father once told me women are the strong ones. I believe it."

His wife leaned down to kiss his mouth. "My mother once told me the greatest power in the world was a kind man. Among your many masculine qualities, it's your hallmark trait. I adore you, Andreas." Her eyes unexpectedly clouded. "I only wish some kindness would spill over on Theo, before it's too late."

How had Theo slipped into this conversation? He couldn't keep up with his wife's thoughts. "Olympia should never have married him."

When Dominique's dark-fringed eyes filled with tears, they darkened to purple, enslaving him. "But then little Ari wouldn't have been born. He's so precious."

"I agree."

Dominique clutched his shoulders. "Theo told me he gave up his parental rights."

Andreas hadn't realized the depth of their conversation.

"Theo's had nothing to do with the baby since he was born. When I went to the hospital to see Olympia, she told me he'd never come near. I'd hoped he would change his mind when he found out the baby was his, but it made no difference."

She choked on a sob. "I was horrified when he told me. I simply can't comprehend anyone abandoning their child. Ari needs his own father. But Theo told me Olympia only married him on the rebound. She'd hurt him terribly."

"What rebound?" Andreas challenged. "Olympia's had a lot of boyfriends, but she hadn't been seriously involved with another man when she met Theo."

"He meant you." Her voice trembled.

"I realize that, but the charge is absurd."

"You mean you never had a relationship with her?"

"A relationship, yes. Through the years she's been like a sister to me—especially with Maris gone. If Theo saw something else, that's his problem."

She bit her lip so enticingly he had to kiss her again.

"It's a tragic problem, Andreas. He's taken his anger and jealousy out on an innocent baby."

"He's not a normal man. Olympia found that out soon after they married."

After a pause, "Did he abuse her?"

"Yes."

"Physically?"

"That, and emotionally. He forbade her to associate

with our family. It was his way of keeping her away from me.''

She sat up against the headboard. "How did she meet him?''

"Through me. Soon after Maris died I took the family out on the yacht. I invited Olympia and her aunt, who raised her, to join us. We spent a couple of weeks together. During that time I still had business to attend to, and would fly back and forth. Theo and I had some commercial interests in common, so I brought him back to the *Cygnus*. He met Olympia. They fell in love and married quickly. You could say it was a whirlwind affair. It turned out to be a mistake I could have prevented.''

"How?''

He shook his head. "I don't know. I should have seen the signs.''

She rubbed his chest. "Obviously no one did. That's usually the way. When we married, you didn't know what a challenge I was going to be.''

"Dominique—'' He covered her hand and squeezed it. "Stop taking on the whole blame. It requires two people to make a marriage. I was so besotted with you. I wanted things perfect and willed them to be that way. In the process I tried to remove every stumbling block before you came to it. But there was one I couldn't avoid, because Olympia swore me to secrecy.''

She rested her head on the pillow next to him. "When you're ready to talk about it, let me know. Right now I want to love the daylights out of you.'' So saying, she hungrily covered his mouth with her own.

Once again this new wife who gave and gave drove

every thought from his head. What remained was their mutual sensual need, which seemed to grow stronger even as it was being appeased.

"I'm coming," Dominique muttered as she entered the penthouse with her arms full of groceries. She rushed to answer the kitchen phone, causing a box of strawberries to fall from the bag. Several of them rolled across the tile floor.

"Hello?" She stooped to pick them up.

"Dominique?"

"Yes?"

"It's Olympia."

"How nice to hear from you."

Dominique couldn't say she was surprised. It was Friday—the start of the weekend. The other woman had said she'd be coming back to Athens and would call. But this soon?

"You sound out of breath. Aren't you well?"

"I'm fine." She brushed off the comment like she would any small irritation, recognizing Olympia said things like that to undermine her confidence. "I just walked in from the market and had a little accident. Are you still in Zakynthos?"

"No. I flew in on the helicopter with Paul this morning, and am back at my aunt's house."

"I bet she missed Ari."

"They were both glad to see each other. That's why I'm phoning. If you don't have any special plans this afternoon, would you like to go shopping with me?"

After the way Andreas had spoiled her, Dominique didn't need to shop for at least a year.

"Another time and I'd love it, but we've invited

Andreas's parents over for dinner this evening. I've got a lot of cooking to do.''

"Where's Maria?"

"She's available for major parties, but tonight I wanted to fix an American meal for them.''

"How interesting.''

Olympia was waiting for an invitation. Making a split-second decision, Dominique decided not to disappoint her. ''Would you like to join us?''

"I wouldn't want to intrude.''

"You won't be. Come—and bring Ari. I'm sure Andreas's parents will enjoy seeing both of you.''

"If you're sure?''

"Of course.''

"What time?''

"Seven.''

"We'll be there. Thank you.''

The minute they clicked off Dominique phoned Andreas at his office. His secretary put her straight through.

"Dominique?''

"Hi, darling.''

"Are you all right?''

That was always the first question to come out of his mouth when they'd been apart, whether it was several hours or a whole day. Hopefully in time his anxiety would lessen to the point that he'd stop.

"I'm fine. Olympia's back in town and I invited her for dinner. I hope that's all right.''

She detected the slightest hesitation before he said, "Did she know we were already having my parents?''

"Yes. To be honest, I thought she sounded a little lonely. Being divorced with a baby has to be hard.

Considering Maris was her best friend, she probably feels at a loss."

"That was very thoughtful of you."

"I have an ulterior motive."

"What's that?"

"I was thinking of inviting someone else who I believe is a little lonely too. But I need his phone number."

"My wife the matchmaker. Dare I ask who it is?"

"Paul."

He muttered something unintelligible.

"Before you tell me it's a bad idea, just hear me out. He's crazy about the baby."

"We're all crazy about Ari."

"Well, you know the old saying—love me, love my child."

"Dominique—they've been friends for years. If something was going to happen between them, don't you think they'd have gotten together long ago?"

"I don't know. Maybe Paul wasn't ready until now."

"What makes you think that?"

"There was a look in his eyes while he was playing with Ari. A tenderness that went beyond a person's normal interest in a baby. What would it hurt to throw the three of them together and let nature take its course?"

"It's fine with me, but I can't vouch for Paul's plans. Would you like me to find out?"

"I think maybe this time the invitation should come from me."

"Instead of the boss?"

"When you put it that way, yes!" She chuckled.

"If *I* ask him, he knows he can turn me down. It'll be an interesting test to see how he reacts."

"Now you've got me intrigued. Here's his number."

She wrote it down on a pad by the phone. Afterward she said, "Don't work too hard. I'll see you this evening."

"What are we having for dinner?"

"Something I guarantee you've never had before."

"In that case I'll be home early for an appetizer— preferably served in the bedroom."

"You're shameless. I'll be waiting."

Euphoric, she hung up, then phoned Paul. He answered on the second ring. No doubt he'd seen the caller ID and thought it was Andreas.

He said something in Greek she didn't quite catch. But one day soon she would understand everything because she'd found a tutor and was going to start lessons on Monday morning.

"Paul? It's Dominique."

"Hi." There was an element of surprise in his tone.

"I was wondering if you have plans for tonight?"

"Nothing I can't get out of. What is it Andreas needs to be done?"

She smiled. "It's what *I* want done. I've invited Olympia and Andreas's parents for dinner at seven. I was hoping you'd come. We're going to watch home movies. I understand you're in ninety percent of them."

The silence lasted so long she thought maybe their connection had broken.

"Paul?"

"I have no interest in Olympia. If I come, you need to know I'm doing it to help you."

A frown creased her brows. "I don't understand."

"I've already said too much. See you at seven."

"Wait—Paul—"

To her chagrin he clicked off, leaving her feeling uneasy on several counts. She knew she wasn't mistaken about his affection for Ari. But it appeared she was way off base about his possible interest in Olympia. In fact he'd reminded her a little of Theo just now.

Why did he think she needed help? Unless it was to smooth the path with Andreas's parents?

She'd never felt closer to her husband. Their reconciliation was working. They were talking, confiding in each other. So far they hadn't reverted back to their old patterns. He was starting to trust her, and she him.

But Paul's cryptic remark worried her. Though she got busy fixing dinner, her lighthearted mood had vanished like the sun slipping behind a giant thunderhead.

Once she'd set the table in the elegant dining room, she hurried to the bedroom to shower and get ready. While she was struggling to zip up the back of her new blue and white jersey print dress, Andreas walked in the bedroom.

"It looks like you need help."

She saw the devilish glint in his eye as he moved toward her. A thrill of excitement coursed through her body.

Instead of finishing the job, he pulled the spaghetti straps off her shoulders and began kissing her nape. His hands kneaded her hips and stomach with restless urgency, turning her legs to mush.

"It's too late for this!" she cried breathlessly, feeling his powerful body brushing against her. "Your parents will be here any minute."

"Don't worry about them. They'll wait for us in the living room."

"We're expecting other guests too."

His hands stilled on her body. "Paul?"

"Yes."

He bit her earlobe gently. "What do you know that I don't?"

Her heart thudded. This was her chance to relate what Paul had said earlier. But instinct told her his remark had only been meant for her to hear.

This evening she would keep her eyes and ears open. Once she and Andreas went to bed, then she would tell him. By that time maybe she would have solved the mystery.

"Don't you know that when a woman is happily married she wants everyone else to be happily married too?"

Her answer must have satisfied him. Andreas closed the zip, then whirled her around. Their mouths met and clung feverishly.

"*Kalispera!*"

"Uh-oh. That's sounds like your father."

"They're early. I bet they've been counting the hours, anticipating this evening."

"I hope so. While you shower, I'll serve drinks."

"Not so fast," Andreas murmured, giving her one more passion-filled kiss before reluctantly letting her go.

She went out to the living room, positive his parents would see the flush on her cheeks.

Once again her appearance created a minor sensation.

The second Andreas's father saw Dominique, his mouth opened. If Eli had been puffing on a cigar, it would have fallen out. He looked like a typical movie producer—horn-rimmed glasses, slightly balding, not quite as tall as his son, but very solid.

She walked over to him and kissed his cheek, then turned to hug Bernice, a striking woman who'd bequeathed her attractive facial features and black hair to her son.

"I'm so glad you could come over tonight. Please sit down. Andreas has only just got home from work and will be out in a minute."

While they found a place for themselves on the couch, she poured them some lime slush from the glass punch bowl she'd placed on the coffee table. Once she'd served them, they complimented her on the taste, but nothing else was forthcoming.

They were too polite and formal, so she decided to plunge in and break the ice.

"I don't know what Andreas has told you, but I want you to know that I love your son, and I've come back to Greece to try to make our marriage work."

His father's black eyes stared hard at her for a moment, reminding her of Andreas. "That's good," he finally said.

"You hurt my Andreas very much when you went away." This from Bernice.

"I hurt myself more," Dominique confessed. "But I had a lot of things to work out."

"My son lost weight in the last year, but you've gained some. You look lovely," the other woman commented. "I know it's early days, but do you think you might be able to give us a grandchild?"

Dominique knew what she was really asking, and reached out to press her arm gently. "I'm cancer-free, and I hope with all my heart that we can have a baby soon."

The news seemed to work a special magic. They both smiled and relaxed, giving her the impression she'd been wrong about their judgment of her. Andreas had insisted her perception of their feelings had been skewed by her own sense of inadequacy. It was humbling to know he'd been right.

Oh…there was a lot of work to be done to help them grow into a close-knit family. Tonight couldn't have come any sooner.

"When our other guests arrive, we'll eat."

Bernice blinked. "Who else is coming?"

"Olympia, for one."

Dominique didn't miss the worried look the two of them exchanged. It was time to clear the air about that.

"Months ago I realized my mistake in not trusting my husband. There's been a lot of pain, but that's behind us now. I know Olympia has been like another member of your family, so I asked her to join us and bring Ari. He's so cute."

"You've seen the baby?" Eli sounded shocked.

"Yes. When I was trying to find Andreas I discovered them on the yacht. Paul's so taken with Ari, I invited him for dinner too. In fact I think they may have arrived. Excuse me for a minute."

She'd heard voices coming from the foyer and went to investigate. Andreas had gotten there ahead of her and escorted the trio into the living room.

He looked particularly sensational in pearl-gray trousers and an open-necked black silk shirt that revealed the dusting of hair on his chest. Her body always melted in an automatic response to his superb male physique.

You'd have thought it had been weeks instead of a few minutes since they'd embraced in the bedroom.

Dominique's gaze traveled to Olympia, who looked stunning in a black print dress that showed off her tanned, voluptuous figure to perfection. Paul wore a cranberry crewneck beneath a cream jacket. He looked good.

But of course it was Ari who stole the show, in a little sailor suit. Bernice reached for him and he didn't even cry. Dominique was jealous. "Everyone help themselves to some slush while I put the dinner on."

Andreas caught her around the waist. "I'll help you."

When they reached the kitchen, he surprised her by backing her up against the wall.

"What are you doing?" she cried breathlessly.

"You look exceptionally beautiful tonight. I think I have to have another appetizer before we eat."

His smoldering kiss made her go limp with desire. She forgot where they were in her need to get even closer to him.

"Oh—excuse me—" Olympia's voice. "I just wanted to put Ari's bottles in the fridge."

Andreas recovered with enviable calm. "Here. I'll take them for you."

Dominique hurried over to the stove, where she could hold on to something until she stopped weaving.

With her husband's help, they got the food on the

table. She urged everyone to come into the dining room. Paul brought Ari in his carrycot and put it on the floor next to Olympia.

Bernice oohed and ahhed over the fresh flowers of the centerpiece. Her reaction augured well for the evening ahead.

It warmed Dominique's heart to watch everyone devour her pot roast—especially Andreas. She'd served it with mashed potatoes, gravy and carrots. The men finished off everything. She had no leftovers, which meant the menu had been a big hit.

Of course Ari's antics dominated the conversation. Delighted at the way the dinner party was going, she got up to serve the strawberry shortcake.

When Eli was through eating, he raised his head. "Dominique? I had no idea you were such a wonderful cook."

"Thank you."

"You could open up your own restaurant in Athens," Paul quipped.

"You know, you really could," Bernice concurred.

Andreas darted Dominique a private thank-you with eyes that gleamed like black jet.

"Where did you find strawberries like these?" Olympia wanted to know.

"At a little market in the Plaka. Their produce is fabulous."

"You'll have to show me."

"I'd be happy to." She looked around. "If everyone's through, Andreas and I have a surprise for you. Come into the study."

By now Ari was awake and wanted a bottle. While

Andreas dealt with warming it, Dominique headed for the other room.

When everyone was seated she said, "I've always wanted to see movies of your family. So I badgered Andreas to get them out of storage. He informs me all of you are in them."

The next two hours were a revelation, punctuated with laughter and tears from Andreas's parents.

He'd arranged the videos in chronological order. They showed him and Maris as babies, at their early birthday parties, at family gatherings with grandparents and extended family. By the time they'd both reached school age Paul and Olympia had begun to figure in many of the scenes.

From the beginning, Dominique had suspected Olympia hero-worshipped Andreas. But the films revealed a definite obsession with him.

Dominique looked around at everyone, riveted to the television screen, wondering if they'd picked up on it. Whenever the pictures included Olympia with the family or friends, she completely ignored the others in order to get Andreas's undivided attention.

One of the later videos showed pictures of them in their twenties. It was painful to watch the way Olympia threw herself at him, parading around in a minuscule bikini.

She was a breathtaking woman, one who could attract any man, but though Andreas had always responded with seemingly good humor, Dominique could tell he wasn't interested. Never once had he initiated anything with her. It underlined his avowal that he'd always thought of her as another sister.

But it was painfully obvious Olympia had always

been determined to get his attention no matter what she had to do. She displayed all the symptoms of a woman who was desperate—and in love.

Something else struck Dominique. Paul had been crazy about Maris. Clearly he'd shown an interest in her at an early age, and she'd appeared to reciprocate his feelings.

After the last video, Andreas turned on the lights. His parents wiped their eyes. They looked from their son to Dominique.

"Thank you for this gift," Eli murmured. "Bernice and I needed to see those pictures again."

"Yes." She patted her chest. "It did my heart good to look at my precious Maris. I didn't think I could stand it, but just the opposite happened. Thank you for a wonderful evening, Dominique."

She rushed across the room to hug both of them. "We'll do it again soon, I promise."

"You'll come to our house next week."

"Yes!" Dominique cried, and gave her another squeeze.

Everyone got up to leave except Olympia. Ari had fallen asleep in her arms.

Paul came over and kissed Dominique's cheek. They walked to the foyer together. "I had no idea Andreas and I were so obnoxious. Thanks for including me."

"It's evident you two have always been joined at the hip. You're welcome here anytime, Paul. I mean it."

"I appreciate that. Dominique—" he whispered, then stopped because the others had come up behind, forcing him to get on the elevator with them. That was the second time he'd tried to tell her something.

Andreas held Ari in his carrycot. He leaned over to nuzzle her neck. "I'll help Olympia to her car and be right back."

"Hurry."

He stepped inside the elevator. But it was Paul's troubled gaze that caught and held hers before the doors closed.

CHAPTER SEVEN

"YOU work fast. After that fabulous meal, I planned to help you with the dishes."

Dominique turned off the kitchen light before running to Andreas. "That isn't what I envisioned for the rest of the night."

He rocked her in his arms, burying his face deep in her hair. "You have no idea what this evening meant to my parents."

"We'll have a lot more of them."

"They left looking happier than I've seen them since before Maris's accident. You're the one who made it all happen," he murmured, kissing the side of her neck. "Reliving memories was cathartic for them."

"It meant a lot to me too. I feel like I know your family so much better than I did."

"You're an integral part of it now. I saw the way they were looking at Ari, anticipating the day when we give them a grandchild."

"Does that mean you'd like us to try for a baby?"

"I wanted to get you pregnant when we first got married, but I was terrified to put you at risk."

"And now?"

"I'll never stop worrying about you, Dominique, but Dr Josephson made me realize a life lived in fear is no life at all."

She pulled away from him enough so she could look

at him. "I'm so glad you said that. Maybe you don't remember, but I've never forgotten what you told me at the altar."

His eyes wandered over her upturned features. "We're going to live all the years God gives us, and rejoice."

"Yes—" she blurted. "You don't know how much I wanted to take those words to heart, but my fears got in the way. That seems such a long time ago. I can hardly relate to the person who ran away at your trial. You have to forgive me for not believing in you, Andreas."

Suddenly lines marred his attractive face. He grasped her hand in a tight grip.

"If you couldn't trust me, it was my fault," he bit out. "I take full responsibility for what happened in those days leading up to the trial. Come on. Let's go in the other room. There's something I have to tell you that can't wait any longer."

Dominique held her breath all the way to the living room.

"This is going to take some time." He urged her to sit down while he remained standing. Whatever was on his mind caused him to pace. This was one time she had to be patient.

"During the time leading up to the trial Olympia swore me to secrecy about something vital. Because it was the pivotal reason Theo brought the adultery case against us, I couldn't tell you everything. No doubt you picked up on it and jumped to the wrong conclusion. I realize now it was a mistake to keep anything from you, so I'm going to break my promise to her and tell you everything. I can't go on letting you assume the blame for the breakdown in our marriage. If I'd been honest with you I have no doubt you would have stuck by me."

Finally Dominique was going to get the answers to some questions that had been crucifying her over the last year. "I guess what I don't understand is how she could expect you to keep a secret from your own wife."

He came to a halt and stared down at her with tortured eyes. "Believe me, I didn't like it. But at the time her reasons made sense to me."

"I see."

She swallowed hard. Olympia's reasons always made sense, but when you took a step back and analyzed them, they were always self-serving for her.

"Our friendship goes back a long way."

"Oh, I know that," she assured him with a little groan. "I saw evidence of it in the videos. It was clear as glass she was infatuated with you from the time she was a girl. It's also obvious she'll be in love with you forever. I never saw anything like it."

Her heart was pounding too fast to be good for her. "Andreas? Were you truly oblivious to her infatuation with you? Or did you realize it and just ignore it, hoping it would go away?"

He rubbed the back of his neck in frustration. "I simply assumed she had a teenage crush that she would eventually outgrow when she started dating other men."

"Did she ever date?"

"Of course."

"Do you recall if she continued to date after Maris was killed?"

"I don't know. I was too grief-stricken to notice much of anything during that period. When Theo fell for her, I was glad. He comes from a good Greek family and is a success in business. Her aunt approved of him. My parents thought he was the perfect person because he was a little older and could handle her strong-willed personality.

"Their marriage seemed to start out on a solid footing. But occasionally Olympia would hint that it was far from perfect. As more revelations unfolded, I grew alarmed. However, I didn't realize how controlling and abusive he could be until after you and I returned to Athens from our honeymoon. Right away I started receiving calls from her. She was afraid of him.

"Usually she phoned me after my work day was over. She was always in tears. I knew she couldn't talk to her aunt about Theo because Mrs. Costas thought he could do no wrong."

"So being the good family friend you are, she chose to confide in you about her marriage?"

"Yes," he muttered grimly.

"That's the reason you started coming home late from the office?"

His hands formed fists at his side. "When I could see a pattern developing, I knew things had to change. I made arrangements for her to see a domestic violence attorney. She didn't dare ask Theo for the money, so I told her I'd pay for it."

"Then you really were convinced he was the one in the wrong?"

"It's not that cut and dried, Dominique. You'll understand why in a minute."

"So, did she take your money and your advice?"

"No. She told me she had too much pride. Furthermore, that Theo would never forgive me if he found out I had helped her. After telling me she was sorry she'd bothered me and would find a way to handle her own problems, she hung up."

"Until the next time?" Dominique couldn't help murmuring.

He nodded. "She didn't phone me for a few days. Then one afternoon, in the middle of an important meeting, I got a frantic phone call from her. She said she needed to see me right away, that it was a matter of life and death."

Dominique's eyes closed tightly. She struggled not to interrupt him.

"I excused myself long enough to go out in the hall, where I could be alone and hear her out. That's when she broke down and told me she'd been raped earlier in the day by an unknown assailant."

"Raped—"

A grimace darkened his features. "It took place in the garage where she'd parked to go to an early morning dentist appointment. When she came out after her checkup, a man dragged her into a corner and assaulted her."

A shudder shook Dominique's body. If it was true, she couldn't imagine anything more terrifying.

"When she had recovered enough to get back in her car, she drove to Acropolis Hospital to report it and be examined. They said they would call her husband to come and get her, but she begged them not to."

"Instead she called you?" Dominique whispered.

"Yes. We both know why. She was already frightened of Theo. She didn't know how he would react. Frankly, neither did I. But I was in the middle of a business merger and couldn't talk to her right then. So I made arrangements for her to be let into my flat. I told her to wait for me until I showed up. On my way over there later, I realized there was only one answer to her problem. She needed to get out of her marriage. Unfortunately she didn't have a brother or a father to turn to.''

Dominique stared up at her husband. ''She didn't need either because she'd always had you.''

''I didn't mind. She was like another sister. If the same thing had happened to Maris I would have moved heaven and earth to protect her from further harm.''

''I understand, darling.''

He took a labored breath. ''When I got there, she was in bed, sobbing.

''Though the hospital had given her a sedative to calm her down, she was still terrified from her ordeal. We talked for a long time. She feared Theo would blame her for getting raped and go into a rage, so she wanted it kept absolutely quiet.

''During that conversation she made me swear I wouldn't tell you, because she knew you and Theo were friends. If you'd found out about the rape, you might have said something to him that could jeopardize her plans to leave him.

''I knew you would never betray her if you were asked to keep her secret,'' Andreas assured her. ''But sometimes it's hard not to give information away in other ways. In your case, your eyes are a barometer of your emotions. If Theo had detected undue concern for Olympia in any way, it might have been enough to set him off. As it was, you and I were having problems communicating. Therefore I thought it best to keep Olympia's rape to myself.

"While we were discussing the best way for her to approach him for a divorce, he burst in the bedroom. To this day I don't know how he managed to get in the flat, but his presence confirmed everything she'd told me about his being out of control."

Too restless to sit, Dominique got to her feet. She hugged her arms to her body.

"Did the rape come up at the trial?"

"No."

She wheeled around. "What?"

"Olympia was terrified Theo's attorney would use it to work against her. Possibly paint her as a promiscuous woman. Though her character isn't anything like that, I was inclined to agree it should be kept secret."

Dominique's body bristled with anger and pain. "So you had to remain silent and take the brunt of Theo's false adultery accusations during the trial?"

"It was all right. I could handle it because I knew the truth." His dark gaze swerved to hers. "As long as I had you at my side, nothing else mattered."

"But you *didn't* have me!" she protested. "I ran out of the courthouse and deserted you." Her breathing had grown shallow. "If I'd known the truth, I would never have left you!"

"Dominique—"

"No—" She spread her hands in despair. "I don't blame you for anything. But it was wrong of Olympia to force you to keep a secret like that from me. I'm so sorry she was raped. I can't imagine anything more horrible. But no matter how much pain she was in, she didn't have the right to ask that of you.''

Heat scorched her cheeks. ''Whether intentionally or not, Olympia relied on your goodness and years of constant friendship to manipulate you into a position that damaged what little communication you and I had going for us.'' Her voice shook.

''Look, Andreas—I've made up my mind to be her friend because of her importance in your life. But what if she gets into another kind of trouble and relies on you to bail her out again? Are you going to fly to her defense without telling me? I can handle anything as long as there's total honesty between us.''

He raked a hand through his hair. ''I swear I'll never hold anything back again.''

His admission didn't make her feel any better. Not when she knew how Olympia operated.

''You say that now, and I believe you, but—''

''But nothing—'' He cut her off before crushing her in his arms. ''I'll make you a promise that anything she has to say to me must be said in front of you too. No exceptions. Not ever again.''

Dominique clung to him, but her heart quaked because he didn't realize how strong a psychological hold Olympia had on him.

By saying what he'd just said, he'd admitted there were going to be more times in the future when Olympia came to him because she was in trouble. Her need of him wouldn't end.

He hadn't seen what Dominique had seen on the films tonight. Olympia's teenage crush had flowered into a womanly obsession. Knowing what Dominique knew now, since dinner, Paul's blunt statement that he could never be interested in Olympia made perfect sense.

Twice since she'd come back to Greece he'd started to say something, then thought the better of it. She had an idea it all had to do with Olympia.

In her office in Sarajevo, when he'd told her Olympia was on board the yacht, she'd thought it had been Paul's way of hurting her because she'd hurt Andreas, his closest friend. But what if it had been a warning?

"Dominique? You're not saying anything. If I thought you didn't believe me..."

Slowly she eased out of his arms. "Yes. Of course I do." She lifted her eyes to his, determined to stay dry-eyed.

"Actually, my mind was on your sister. Tonight it was apparent to me from the videos that Paul and Maris had a strong attraction for each other. Every time the camera zoomed in on him he was staring at her, and she would respond with laughter and long yearning looks."

He studied her face intently. "We all grew up together, but neither one of them ever discussed their feelings for each other with me. As we got older, they both dated other people."

She smoothed a strand of hair off her face. "Don't you find it odd that neither of them were married by the time Maris was involved in that accident?"

A frustrated sound came out of his throat. "Paul's his own man. Most of our friends didn't marry till their late twenties or early thirties. I never gave it any thought. As for Maris, I didn't think any of the guys she met measured up to her.''

"Did you tell her that?''

"Only with a few of them. It's a brother thing. I believed that one day the right man would come into her life and that would be it.''

"Something tells me Paul was that man.''

His eyes flashed in pain. "If that's true, then I don't know why in the hell he didn't say something to me years ago!''

"Maybe he was afraid of your reaction. Perhaps he thought you might not approve.''

"That's not possible. He's the best man I know.''

"I'm afraid he may be the last person who knows it.''

He kneaded her shoulders urgently. "You're serious?''

"Yes. Until recently I didn't realize how really sweet and shy he is.''

"Paul?'' Her husband was incredulous.

"Yes. He hides it behind a stony façade, but I saw through it when he was playing with Ari.''

"He doesn't have any trouble finding women.''

."Except for the one he wanted,'' she whispered.

Andreas groaned.

"Darling—do you remember when you entered the bedroom at the villa and teased him about having hidden talents?''

"What about it?''

"He was turned away from you so you couldn't see him, but his face went red because you'd caught him in a tender moment, interacting with the baby. It was very revealing. I saw a whole new side to him I hadn't realized was there. I bet he's been silently grieving for Maris all this time and no one knew it. Tonight while we were watching the videos, I watched his face. His eyes were glued to Maris the entire time.''

''He should have told me,'' Andreas muttered in a tortured voice.

''It was too long ago, and you couldn't have done anything about it,'' she said. ''But maybe sometime you might ask him if it's true. It's possible he'll unburden himself. I'm thinking it might be a relief to him. Like Olympia's secret, that drove such a wedge between us, his secret may have deprived him of ultimate happiness with Maris. Tonight was good for your parents, but I got the feeling Paul left the penthouse with a heavy heart.''

He stared hard at her for a minute. ''What else did my brilliant wife see tonight in those videos that I didn't?''

''A handsome little boy who grew up into a gorgeous, vital man. One who I can't believe saved himself for me,'' she admitted in a tremulous voice.

Andreas lifted her face to him. ''I love you, Dominique. You're my very life. Come to bed with me. I want to show you over and over again what you mean to me. I need you, darling, now more than ever.''

How long had she waited to hear those words and know he really meant them...?

Monday morning, Dominique left her tutor's office at the University of Athens with an armful of assignments. Next she took a taxi to Acropolis Hospital, where she arranged to meet with the head of volunteers to talk about her new project.

During a party on Saturday night, that she and Andreas had hosted for some prominent businessmen and their wives, he had surprised her by announcing that his wife was going to head a new cancer foundation center.

It had been his way of letting her know she could depend on his full support, even if it was still hard for him to deal head-on with the subject.

Nothing could have thrilled her more. Their marriage was going to work. She just knew it.

But there was one person she wanted to talk to.

Before she left the hospital, she phoned Paul and asked him to meet her for lunch. He must have sensed it was important, because he didn't hesitate to join her at a little café near the hospital.

She got there first, and ordered juice while she waited for him. Always prompt, he approached her table before long and sat down to peruse the menu.

After the waiter came and they'd both ordered salad, he said, "Thank you for inviting me the other night. You're an excellent cook."

She smiled. "I don't mind hearing that twice. But compliments weren't the reason I wanted to see you."

"I didn't think so. What's going on?"

"Paul—" She stared at him. "Did you know Olympia was raped?"

The silence between them lasted a long time. Eventually he said, "I didn't know about the rape until months after you'd gone back to Sarajevo."

"So my husband kept it from you too?"

"I doubt he would ever have told me, but we had a fight over you and it finally came out."

"You fought over me?"

"Yes. I told him he was a fool not to go after you and beg you to come back to him. He was bitterly angry at the time, and said that if you didn't have enough faith in him and his love for you, then it was too late for your marriage.

"That's when I told him that if I'd been in your shoes I would have done the same thing and left him too. One thing led to another. We traded verbal blows until he finally admitted that there were things I didn't know—things he'd had to keep a secret from you. When he told me about the rape, I told him he was an idiot to have ever believed anything Olympia told him."

Dominique blinked. "Then you don't think she was really raped?"

"Do you?" he fired back.

"Frankly, no."

"Then we're in agreement. Think about it, Dominique. She swore him to secrecy, yet she never told Theo. She refused to let it come up at the trial. It was the perfect lie. She put Andreas in a box he couldn't get out of, knowing it would impact heavily on you."

"You're right."

"I asked Andreas if he'd checked with the hospital. He said he didn't have to. Olympia would never make up a lie like that."

"Oh, Paul." She shook her head.

"When I could see that he was firmly entrenched

in his belief, I realized there was nothing more I could do.''

She bit her lip. ''You were trying to warn me about her before I boarded the yacht, weren't you?''

He nodded.

''Those videos were a revelation, Paul. But I'm afraid my husband can't see he's her obsession.''

''I *know* he is,'' Paul muttered. ''She hates me because I've been on to her for a long time. She stays away from me as much as possible. When she realized you'd invited me for dinner, she must have been livid. It meant I'd be watching for any tricks she decided to pull.''

Dominique buried her face in her hands. ''She's not about to go away. I don't know what to do. Since coming back to Greece I've decided to play along. The other night Andreas promised me he'll never keep secrets from me again.''

''He means it.''

''I know, but—''

''But you don't trust Olympia any more than I do. She's the one who abused Theo, not the other way around. If you want my opinion, she planned it so he would find her and Andreas together.''

Her head shot up. ''You're kidding!''

''No. The only reason she married him was for additional security.''

''That's what Theo said.''

''I imagine it didn't take him long to realize Olympia was using him. Mrs. Costas is on a fixed income. With her health slowly fading, Olympia decided she needed someone to foot the medical bills if she required extended hospitalization.''

"She used him."

"Olympia doesn't have a conscience that I can see. When Andreas didn't succumb to her wiles, she married Theo. But she made certain her relationship with Andreas never changed. Not long after that he met you and fell in love. I could tell she was consumed by jealousy. It drove her to cause problems both before and after your marriage."

Dominique reflected on those moments. "I didn't want to believe she could be so cruel, but there were times…"

"She's a dangerous person. But, no matter what she did, Andreas only had eyes for you. It's my belief she intentionally enflamed Theo so that he wouldn't only divorce her, he would charge them with adultery. Anything to make it as ugly as possible, so Theo would give her a settlement but want nothing more to do with her."

"Then she achieved her goal," Dominique said sadly. "I went to see Theo at his office."

"When?"

"The day you and I flew to Athens—after we left Zakynthos. He told me he gave up his parental rights."

"I can't say I blame him. To try to work out visitation with a woman like that would be hell on earth."

"Poor Ari. He's so sweet and innocent."

"I don't like it any more than you do, but Olympia's not normal."

"That's what Andreas said about Theo."

"Because Andreas is blind when it comes to Olympia. She's always known how to play the victim. Throughout their lives she used Maris to get to him."

"In what way?"

"She'd make remarks about how lucky Maris was to have a father and brother who always looked out for her. Olympia knew exactly what she was doing. She conned Andreas, and she conned Theo until he proposed. But as soon as she didn't want him anymore she knew how to get rid of him."

The picture Paul was painting made a horrible kind of sense, but it struck new fear in Dominique's heart.

"Can you think of a better way for it to end than the way it did in that trial?" Paul asked. "Especially when Andreas felt sorry for her because of the rape. She knew that if Theo abandoned her Andreas would always take care of her."

"I'm afraid he always will." Dominique's voice trembled.

"Olympia planted those seeds early on and they took root. Andreas would have to be presented with proof that she lied to him about the rape in order for the blinders to come off."

"That would be next to impossible, Paul," she half sobbed. "My husband's the kind of man who believes in a person's innocence until they're proven guilty. I don't want to believe all these horrible things about Olympia, but when I was talking to Theo he denied having said certain things about me. He called her a liar."

"That comes as no surprise. I really feel sorry for him. But you know what frightened me most?"

She blinked back her tears. "What?"

"The first time I met you, I was afraid she would make mincemeat of you. I've never seen a man fall as hard for a woman as Andreas did for you. He was never the same again and Olympia knew it. She despised you for it. I knew in my gut there was going to be trouble. Andreas couldn't see it. He was too happy, too in love. But in his way, he'd abandoned Olympia.''

''In her eyes, I'm sure you're right. But of course he couldn't have known what he'd done. He's told me repeatedly she doesn't mean anything more to him than a close friend of his sister.''

Paul nodded. ''He assumed she was happy in her marriage to Theo. He didn't realize how devastated she was when he got married. He still didn't figure it out when Olympia managed to get you to invite her and Theo on the yacht for those little weekend get-togethers. You were on your honeymoon, yet she played on your goodness, Dominique. She knew you would do anything for Andreas. You were all puppets dancing on her strings.''

She took a fortifying breath. ''Not anymore we're not. Forewarned is forearmed.''

Paul reached out to squeeze her hand. ''I'm glad. You're the best thing that ever happened to Andreas. You'll never know my surprise and delight when you told me you were going to fly back to Greece with me. I had a feeling in my gut your intention was to try to save your marriage.''

''I love him so much.''

He smiled. ''That's obvious.''

''Thank you for being my friend. Andreas loves you without question. Now I know why. With you on my side, I won't let Olympia win.''

''Are you going to confront her?''

She eyed him narrowly. ''Not unless she forces me. One thing is certain: there won't be any more secrets.''

"Are you going to tell Andreas we met for lunch?"

"Of course. In fact I was hoping to ride back to the office with you and surprise him."

He looked relieved. "Then let's go." He started to pay the bill, but she threw down the money. "Nope—this is my treat."

Paul helped her up from the table. "I know the boss. He's going to love it when you pop in. You've never done anything like that before."

"There are so many things I never did before. I don't know how our marriage lasted four months."

"Yes, you do," he murmured. "You and Andreas have the real thing going for you."

Paul was a sweetheart.

He rang for a taxi. Before long they reached the building and rode the elevator to the top floor.

Like a girl anticipating her first date, she felt her heart skittering all over the place as she followed him past a pool of secretaries to the door of Andreas's private suite. The rooms were very light and contemporary. He loved the sun.

When the two of them walked in, he was standing at the window talking on the phone. Paul gave a knuckle rap, causing Andreas to look around.

She'd purposely worn a soft lemon outfit with a fitted short-sleeved jacket Andreas had admired when they'd gone shopping. To humor him she'd tried it on, and he'd said she looked good enough to eat.

That was how she wanted him to feel now that they'd walked in his office unannounced.

When he saw her, a slow smile broke out on his impossibly handsome face. His conversation ended in short order and he hung up.

"You two look like the cat who swallowed the pro-verbial canary. What's going on?"

"I took Paul to lunch."

"Without me?"

"It was my special thank-you to him for coming all the way to Sarajevo on a terrible mission to save you and me from destruction. He's been a true friend to both of us. I'm very grateful." Her voice wobbled.

"So am I," Andreas murmured.

Paul's face went red again.

"Oh—here, darling." She put a sack on his desk. "I brought you a pastry to feed your sweet tooth. It was my dessert, but I decided to give it to you. I've got to start working out in a gym so I'll be in shape to run some marathons."

"We've got one downstairs on the third floor. Use it all you want. When I can arrange it, I'll work out with you."

"I'd love that."

"So would I," he said, before he retrieved the bak-lava from the sack and promptly devoured it.

Paul eyed both of them in amusement. "I've got work waiting for me. See you two later." He left the room, closing the door behind him.

Andreas's gaze traveled over her with heartstopping intimacy. "What are you doing way over there?" he whispered. "We don't have much time before I have to go into a big meeting."

She put her things down on his desk, then hurried around to him. He molded her to him, running his hands over her back with increased urgency while re-warding her with a long, hungry kiss.

When he finally relinquished her mouth, their lips

more or less stuck together. She started to giggle. "You're covered in honey."

He grinned. "So are you…now."

"I should have brought you cake."

"You're here. That's all that matters. Now maybe I'll be able to make it through the rest of the day."

"Oh, Andreas—" She hugged him tighter around the waist. "I love you so much I can hardly breathe when you hold me. When I think of the year we've spent apart…"

"I do believe you're beginning to understand how I feel. Do you have any idea how many times I stood at these windows, looking out over the city, wishing you'd sweep into my office and tell me you were back to stay?"

"I wanted to, darling. Every minute I was away from you was agony."

He rocked her harder. "When I sent Paul to Greece with the papers, I wanted to hear that you'd thrown them back in his face. But you did something much more wonderful. You came home with him."

She kissed the cleft in his chin. "Yes, and then you promptly told me to sign them because you never wanted to see me again. But I knew why, and it was my turn to be terrified that you really meant it–and might not follow me to Zakynthos. Thank heaven you did!"

His mouth closed over hers with smothering force. Dominique almost forgot where they were. If anyone were to walk in on them…

She finally tore her lips from his. "I wish we could go home right now, but I know you've got a meeting so I'd better leave."

"Not so fast. What's your Greek teacher like?"

"He's young and handsome and single," she said with a straight face.

"You little witch," he growled into her neck. "I want to know how your first formal lesson went."

"Well, I can say *Ohi, ya, yasou, kalimera, kalispera, kalinihta, ti kanis, poly kala*—and I know what they mean. Want to try me?"

As rich laughter burst out of him, his private secretary buzzed him. "Kyrie Stamatakis?"

"Is everyone assembled in the conference room?"

"Except for Mr. Kazarian, who just phoned to let me know he's on his way from the bank."

"Let me know when he arrives."

"Of course. And you have a phone call on line two. It's Olympia Panos. She says it's urgent."

CHAPTER EIGHT

As IF a shadow had passed across the face of the sun, Andreas's smile faded. On cue, Dominique's happiness evaporated.

"You'd better take it, darling."

She moved out of his arms and sat down in front of his desk, wondering what was so pressing that Olympia should interrupt Dominique's husband on a busy work day.

How come she hadn't called on his cellphone? Had she been afraid Andreas wouldn't answer it right away? Or had she purposely planned to go through his secretary so he'd be forced to deal with her immediately?

On the heels of her chat with Paul, Dominique was all ears.

Andreas picked up the receiver to talk to her. Whatever Olympia had to say didn't last long. After telling her he'd work something out, he hung up, looking concerned.

"What's wrong?"

"Olympia's aunt has developed a pain that won't go away. The doctor wants her to go into the clinic. If Olympia drives her, she's going to need help with Ari. I'll send Paul."

"Don't you need him for the meeting?"

"I'll ask my secretary to take notes."

"Andreas—do you mean to tell me Olympia doesn't have a sitter she can call in an emergency?"

What a convenient bind to be in, so that Andreas would have to drop whatever he was doing and run to her assistance.

"It's my understanding that Olympia's aunt usually tends him if she needs help."

"Well, I'm free for the rest of the day. Call your driver and he can take me over to her apartment right now. You can join me after work. How does that sound?"

"You don't mind?"

"Heavens, no. I've been dying to get my hands on him, and scrunch that cute little body of his."

He smiled. "You'd be saving my life."

"Then it's settled. What's her address?"

He wrote it on a piece of paper, then came around and handed it to her with a hard, swift kiss. "I'll be by later."

"I can't wait!"

She grabbed her things off the desk. He walked her out to the elevator and gave her one more kiss before the doors closed.

When she stepped outside the building a limo was waiting for her. She showed the driver the paper, then got in the back and they took off.

Downtown traffic in Athens was pure chaos at the lunch hour. She lay back against the seat, thankful someone else was at the wheel. It took a native-born son to know how to dodge cars and navigate through this huge city which was still relatively new to her.

Besides all the monuments and museums, it would

take years to explore all the little side streets and historical districts.

In less than ten minutes they came to a newer residential area with more modern-looking buildings. The chauffeur let her out in front of a five-story apartment. Apparently Olympia and her aunt lived on the third floor.

She thanked the driver and hurried inside. After finding the right button on the wall, she buzzed it and waited for the elevator.

Half a minute later she emerged and walked down the hall. Andreas had indicated it was the second door on the left. Dominique pressed the bell.

Within seconds Olympia opened the door. A surprised cry escaped her to see Dominique standing there.

"Where's Andreas?"

Paul had asked her if she was going to confront Olympia. This was as good a time as any.

"He has a big meeting this afternoon, Olympia. You had no business calling him. Now that you have a baby, you need to find some sitters you can phone at a moment's notice. Since I happened to be at his office when your call came through, I offered to come and tend Ari."

"It's difficult to find someone you can trust," Olympia said, without revealing the least bit of embarrassment. Dominique's father would call Olympia a cool customer.

"I'm afraid you're going to have to."

"Ari doesn't do well with strangers."

"No baby does," Dominique rejoindered. "But there are hundreds of thousands of single moms out there who manage to get help and do just fine. I'm sure you will too once you try. However, I'm here now, and I can drive all of you to the clinic. Or, if you'd prefer, I'll stay here with Ari while you go with your aunt.''

Clearly this wasn't the way Olympia had envisioned things turning out.

''Ari cries with you.''

''Give me a little time with him and he'll be fine.''

''I don't know…'' She looked fit to be tied.

''Please don't worry. I promise I'll do everything I can for him until you get back.''

''Come in, then.''

At last.

Dominique followed her into the living room, where her aunt was seated on the edge of a chair, her breathing strained. The older red-haired woman only knew a little English. After meeting her at the wedding, this was only the second time Dominique had seen her.

''Hello, Mrs. Costas. Do you remember me?''

''Yes.''

''I'm sorry you're not feeling well. I've come to watch Ari.''

''He is sleeping.''

''I'll take good care of him while you go see the doctor.''

''That's very kind of you. Thank you.''

''You're very welcome.''

Olympia hurried back in the living room. ''His bottles are in the fridge. He's due to wake up for one in a half-hour. Then he'll play for a while. Unless this is something serious with my aunt, I hope to back for his next bottle, which will be around five.''

''You go, and don't worry about anything. If you need me to stay over tonight, I can.''

''Thank you,'' her aunt murmured again.

Nothing from Olympia.

Dominique saw them out the door, then tiptoed through the apartment to the tiny third bedroom where Ari lay sleeping. He looked like a little dark-haired angel.

She went back to the living room, deciding this would be a good time to do her homework for the next day. There was a small table in the kitchen where she could study.

Along with her textbook was a tape to help with her pronunciation. She put it in the little mini pocket recorder she'd purchased and began imitating the words of the first lesson.

After about forty-five minutes Ari started to cry. She jumped up from the table to warm his bottle in a pan of hot water. When she'd gotten that started, she hurried down the hall, calling out his name so he would be alerted that a stranger was in the house.

At first he cried his heart out when he saw her. But after she'd walked around the apartment with him, patting his back while she sang some songs to him, he settled down. Several times his lower lip quivered, but when she started to feed him his bottle, he took to it and drank noisily.

She put a diaper over her shoulder to burp him. He was a good boy and did everything he was supposed to do. Once he'd digested, she found his little floor gym and took it in the living room so he could play.

He focused for a long time on the toys. Even after a diaper change he kept kicking everything, and got so excited his little fists wound around like a boxer's.

Oh, he was cute.

"You're making me hungry for my own baby, Ari. Do you know that?"

Dominique blew on his tummy. It made him smile. He even laughed once.

It hurt her to think about his mother. Olympia had problems. If she didn't get some professional help to deal with her obsession with Andreas she was going to get worse. Ari shouldn't have to grow up with a mom that troubled.

She obviously kept a neat, lovely home. The baby looked perfect. Olympia was a beautiful woman. An outsider looking in would see nothing wrong with this picture.

Andreas certainly couldn't.

He was so used to standing in for her the way a brother would he thought nothing of leaving work to come and help her out. This couldn't go on. Dominique refused to allow it—otherwise their marriage *would* be destroyed.

The day wore on, but there was no word from Olympia yet. Dominique warmed another bottle and began feeding it to Ari. While she was burping him she heard the bell ring.

With Ari slumped against her shoulder she walked to the front door and looked through the peephole. Her heart raced at discovering Andreas standing there.

"Who is it?" she called out deliberately.

"Your lord and master."

"Are you sure? Mine's supposed to be at work."

"He got off early."

"How come?"

"Because he wanted to be with his wife."

"Well, in that case—"

She opened the door. He swept in and embraced them both. When Ari saw who it was, his precious face beamed and he reached for him.

Dominique did a fake pout. "I'm jealous. Here I've tended him all afternoon, and he wants you."

Andreas kissed his cheeks. "We're buddies—aren't we, Ari?"

"I love him. He makes me want a baby of our own so badly I can hardly stand it."

"As soon as Olympia gets back we'll go home and I'll try my best to accommodate your wishes. According to my calculations, you should be ovulating right now."

"I hope I am."

"What else have you been doing this afternoon?"

"Studying. But I didn't get a lot done once he woke up."

"Let's take a look at your homework."

They walked into the kitchen. She held her breath while he examined the material in her notebook.

When he lifted his head, his eyes were gleaming. "Not one mistake. I'm very impressed, *agape mou*."

"Well, I did live here for four months."

One dark brow dipped. "I've known Americans who've lived here for years. They may be fluent, but they can't write our language."

He always made her feel good. "How did your meeting go?"

She noticed the triumphant glint in his eye. "Very well."

"Good. That means you'll be able to keep a roof over our heads for one more day anyway."

At her comment they both laughed. That was how Olympia found them when she walked in the kitchen.

"Olympia—" Dominique said. "How's your aunt?"

The other woman's eyes had centered on Andreas, even though Ari was trying to reach for his mother.

"She has pleurisy, but the doctor says she's going to be all right. I told her to go lie down."

"I'm glad it's nothing too serious," Andreas murmured.

Dominique eased the baby into his mother's arms. "My grandmother once had the same thing. It's very painful, but if your aunt's careful she'll recover."

"I hope Ari didn't cry the whole time," she said, without acknowledging Dominique's remarks.

"No. He fussed a little when he first saw me, but everything was perfect after that. He's had two bottles."

"Thank you."

"I was happy to watch him. He's so good I can tell you're a wonderful mother."

"You are, Olympia," Andreas concurred. "You manage better than most women with husbands."

Though Andreas had meant well, Dominique could imagine how Olympia cringed inwardly at that remark. "Excuse me and I'll get my things out of the kitchen." She left them standing there to talk.

In two seconds she was back, and waited for him at the front door. Something drastic needed to happen for the situation to change, but at the moment Dominique was out of ideas.

Another minute and they'd left for the penthouse in the limo. He squeezed her hand. "Shall we order from the deli and eat dinner in bed?"

"That sounds divine."

He pulled her against him and kissed her throat. "You were wonderful to tend Ari like that today. I realize Olympia's not demonstrative, but I know she appreciated it."

"She thanked me. But let's face it, Andreas. Now that her aunt is getting ill more frequently she can't expect you or Paul to solve her problems."

"I don't intend to. I'm thinking of hiring a permanent nanny to help her."

"Do you think that's wise?" she asked, before she could stop herself.

"What do you mean?"

She averted her eyes. "Can't you see she's becoming more and more dependent on you? Every time you do something for her, she'll turn to you the next time she needs something else. That's how people are. If Olympia is going to make it in this world, she has to work through her problems by herself until she becomes strong."

"She doesn't have your inner strength, Dominique."

"Andreas—as long as someone has always been there to make certain she got picked up the second she stumbled, she hasn't had an opportunity to find out what she's capable of on her own."

"But with a sick aunt and a new baby on her hands, she needs help."

Paul had been right. Olympia had played the victim so long Andreas wasn't aware how deeply he'd bought into it.

She didn't bring up the subject of Olympia again until later, after they'd eaten souvlaki and cheesecake in bed. Once the news on the TV was over, there wasn't anything Andreas wanted to watch. He turned it off and removed their trays.

Then he flashed her a smile that turned her heart over. "We don't want any accidents like we had last time."

She chuckled. "No, we don't."

"I've been looking forward to this moment since you deserted me at the office," he said, climbing under the covers. He rubbed his hand up and down her arm as a prelude to making love.

Normally she would have reached for him, but she'd made up her mind they had to talk about Olympia. This situation with her couldn't go on another day. Discussing everything with Paul had given her courage.

"Darling?"

"Hmm?"

"Can we talk for a minute?"

"Of course." He rolled on his side next to her and propped his head in his hand. "I can tell something important is on your mind." His other hand continued to caress her arm and shoulder.

"I want to tell you about the conversation Paul and I had today."

"Sounds like it was a long one."

"Not really. Do you remember how you and I

promised there would be no more secrets between us?"

"What do you think?"

"I mean *not any*?"

He stopped the motion of his hand and simply rested it on the inside of her elbow. "This sounds serious."

"It is. Very. I believe our marriage is doomed if we don't address a certain issue right away."

He made a protesting sound in his throat.

"I realize you don't want to talk about this, but we have to."

"For the love of heaven, Dominique—just say what you have to say." In the next breath he'd levered himself from the bed and had shrugged into his bathrobe, which had been lying over the footboard.

"It isn't that easy. You're already defensive and I haven't even told you anything yet."

"Except that our marriage is doomed," he lashed out emotionally.

"Only if we don't resolve a problem that's been staring us in the face since I first met you."

He sucked in his breath. "I'm listening."

"Olympia's in love with you."

"We've already had this discussion."

"Paul believes she was lying about the rape. I tend to agree with him."

"Give me one compelling reason why you believe it too."

"Because you've been her obsession for years. It's something she'll never get over without professional help."

"You and Paul think she needs a psychiatrist?"

"Yes."

He bit out an epithet.

"Darling— I don't know if you can, but I wish you could step back for one minute and look at what happened today objectively. A young, beautiful, divorcee mother, who isn't your wife or a family member, called you at your office. You're an important businessman who's attempting to reconcile with your wife. She knows all this, yet she actually asked you to drop everything to come to her rescue. She didn't go through your wife. She didn't even try."

Dominique couldn't tell if he'd already closed off, but she had to try to get through to him.

"I want you to think of all the married men who were at our party the other night. How many of them have young, beautiful, divorcee mothers phoning them during critical business transactions and expecting them to do their bidding, with their wives not knowing anything about it?"

He shook his head. "I can't be objective about it, Dominique. She's a family friend."

"One you've elevated to the status of sister. But that isn't enough for her, because she wants to be your wife! Since that's an impossibility, she's out to sabotage any relationship to keep you in her life. She got rid of Theo, and she almost got rid of me. But I came back to Greece to fight for my marriage, so she's applying new tactics."

"Give me an example."

"All right. First I'd like to know something—did you include her aunt in your invitation when you told her the yacht and the villa at Zakynthos were at her disposal?"

"Of course."

"Then how come Mrs. Costas wasn't there when I went aboard?"

"Olympia told me she'd decided to stay with her nephew."

"Her aunt has a nephew?"

"Yes. He's married with children."

"That's news to me. Where does he live?"

"In Athens."

"Then it's very interesting that Olympia should call *you* to help her with her aunt when there's a nephew nearby."

"He's rarely available."

"How do you know? Have you talked to him personally?"

The silence from her husband was illuminating.

"Tell me something else. How long was her vacation supposed to be?"

His breathing sounded labored. "Until the end of September."

"So how come she came back this last weekend?"

"I don't know."

"Did you promise to take your vacation with her?"

He impaled her with a piercing gaze. "You know I didn't. I only flew out there for a few days, to make sure everything was running smoothly."

"Yet, according to you, her vacation isn't supposed to be over for three weeks. Don't you find it odd that she should cut it short by twenty-one days and then call me the second she returned to Athens on Friday, wanting to go shopping?"

"She and Maris used to love it."

"Doesn't she have any friends her own age?"

"Of course."

"If she's lived here all her life, how come *I'm* the only person she could think of to spend an afternoon with?"

For once he had no response.

"She knew you and I had been separated for a year, that we craved private time together. What kind of a family friend intrudes on something so personal with total disregard for our feelings? For that matter, what kind of family friend would show up every weekend of our honeymoon on the yacht? Or did you invite her and never tell me?"

Again, silence.

"Most grooms I know don't want to see any family members or old friends on their honeymoon. Would Maris have intruded? I hardly think so. Andreas—I'm not saying these things to be mean or cruel. All I want you to do is think about her behavior. If you go on letting her be the third party in our marriage, it won't work. A man and wife are supposed to cleave to each other. There's no room in there for anyone else.

"Though I'd hoped never to have to tell you this, Olympia was extremely insensitive to me when we met. She put unkind words in Theo's mouth, insinuating that you were courageous to marry me, that most men would have a problem with a woman like me."

"She actually said those things to you?" Andreas demanded harshly.

"Yes. Those things and much more. Little insidious comments about me being too young and unsophisticated for you. She never talked to me if it wasn't something to do with my cancer. Was I feeling all right today? Did I think I could handle marriage considering I might have to face another mastectomy down the road? Was it really fair to marry you knowing there would be a death sentence hanging over our marriage?''

He swore savagely. Maybe she was reaching him after all.

''I've never known a really mean-spirited person before. I assumed it had to be her extreme jealousy that brought out the worst in her. But I never imagined she'd go so far as to turn Theo against you. Didn't you ever wonder why he became so upset he felt driven to shame you in court? You were business friends. I found his actions totally out of character. Because Olympia lived with him, I believe she played a major role in that.

''She knew what she was doing when she swore you to secrecy about the rape. It bound you to her in a new way that gave her power. It's my opinion she'll continue to work on you unless you put a stop to it. You're the only one who can.

''I've only been in Greece a week, and already she has infiltrated our family dinner and called you at your office, begging for help. What's next, Andreas? A phone call in the middle of the night because she wants you to come over and see what's wrong with Ari?

''All she has to do is ask, and you come running. It's because for years and years you've been programmed to respond that way, and she knows it. Only she's not a teenager anymore. Her ploys are growing more desperate. If you can't see that every time she calls, it's an excuse to be with you, then what hope do we have?'' she cried. "I don't ever want to leave you, but I'll have to if something doesn't change."

His mouth had gone white around the edges.

"You know how much I love you, Andreas. I came back to fight for you—for us. But she's always there, right in the middle. We can't possibly think about making future plans or having a baby under these circumstances."

She'd promised herself she wouldn't break down, but the tears fell anyway.

"Dominique—"

She heard his unspoken entreaty. For once she couldn't respond to it.

"If you don't mind, I'd prefer we don't make love for a while. I *could* be ovulating. Even with protection, mistakes happen. As I said before, our marriage needs to be on firm ground if we're going to become parents. Until Olympia is out of our lives, it's never going to happen."

Dominique had delivered her ultimatum. But she was counting on him to grab her and assure her she would never have to worry about Olympia again.

To her horror, seconds turned into minutes. Then he disappeared from the bedroom.

Another nightmare had begun—much worse than before.

"Paul?"

"Andreas—"

"Are you alone?"

"No. Give me five minutes and I'll call you back."

If he was with a woman, Andreas hated interrupting him, but this was one night he had to have answers.

Just now Dominique had managed to paint a picture he could never have imagined. It had shaken him to the foundations. Certain beliefs he'd held as core truths all his life were on the verge of disintegrating.

Not only his best friend, but the woman he loved more than life, were convinced Olympia had a dark side. As dark as the night surrounding him.

The second his cellphone rang, he answered it.

"I'm free now. Go ahead, Andreas."

"I'm sorry to have disturbed you. Paul—I have so many questions to ask, I don't know where to start first. So I'll just bludgeon my way through. Earlier today Dominique told me she believed you were in love with Maris. Is that true?"

When he didn't answer, it was all Andreas needed to know.

"How long were you in love with her?"

"Since high school," his friend finally admitted.

His eyelids squeezed together. "Did you ever tell her how you felt?"

"No. I told Olympia, and asked her to put in a good word for me."

Bile rose in his throat.

"What was the feedback?"

"She said it would be better if I didn't know. It could hurt me."

A groan escaped, rocking Andreas on his feet. "You've answered all my questions but one. When did you figure out Olympia?"

"Not until I happened to overhear her talking to Dominique, right before you got married. They were in the vestibule of the church and didn't know I happened to be on the stairs. Olympia asked her how she would dare undress in front of you once you were married.''

Andreas felt a stabbing pain in his chest. ''I don't know what to say, Paul.''

''It's too late for regrets. Because of Maris's accident, I can't believe we were destined to be together. But it's not too late for you.''

''I'm going to catch Olympia in the act.''

''That shouldn't be too difficult. She's doesn't have a clue you've finally caught on to her. Within the next few days she'll drum up something new.''

''When she does, I'll be waiting for her.''

''Have you told Dominique yet?''

''No. I'm not going to say anything until Olympia's out of our lives for good. My wife has suffered long enough.''

''We've all suffered. Have you got a strategy?''

''Yes.''

''Do you need help?''

''Yes. Have you got a half an hour?''

''If it's to plan a way to get rid of Olympia, I'm all yours for as long as it takes.''

CHAPTER NINE

DOMINIQUE entered the gym the next morning after her language class, ready for a workout. Several well-cut males lifting weights called out hello to her in English. Andreas had once told her that her walk was so American, her nationality stuck out a mile.

"Hi, guys."

A buff-looking hunk approached her with a smile. "I'm Alex, the manager and trainer." His eyes swept over her in masculine admiration. "I've never seen you in here before, or I would have remembered."

"You're right. This is my first time." She looked around at the state-of-the-art equipment. There were only half a dozen men taking advantage of the facilities. "Where are all the women?"

"They usually come at the end of the day. Are you here to sign up for a membership?"

"My husband has one."

"What a shame." He frowned. "Every guy in here is going to be sorry to hear that." She chuckled. "What's the lucky man's name?"

"Andreas Stamatakis."

In an instant his expression sobered. He let out a low whistle. "You're his first wife?"

With that question, Dominique realized how pervasive the gossip had been following the trial.

"I'm his one and only wife." But maybe not for long.

His hands went to his hips. "I meant no disrespect. In fact that came out wrong."

"Don't worry about it. I know what you meant. We were separated for a year, but now I'm back. My name's Dominique."

"That's a beautiful name. French, isn't it?"

"Yes. My mother studied in France and fell in love with the name."

This time his inspection of her was professional. "You are in excellent shape. I take it you're no stranger to a gym?"

"I've practically lived in one for the last year and a half."

"Then—please. Make yourself at home. The dressing room is back there." He pointed to a doorway behind him.

"Thank you."

She passed through to the locker room. After putting her hair in a ponytail, she emerged minutes later in her running shorts and top, ready to do her stretches. Dominique liked to get in her workouts early. They energized her for the rest of the day.

Ignoring the men's interested gazes, she ran through her routine, which included dumbbell bench presses to strengthen her arms and upper body. Finally she got on the treadmill and put herself through the paces.

Even if she couldn't do anything about Olympia, she could do this for herself. It felt good to be in control of her body. The discipline worked hand in hand with her mind, keeping her thoughts focused on what was important.

"That's it," she muttered to herself.

A few more stretching exercises and she was ready

for a shower. Once dressed, in a skirt and blouse, she brushed out her hair and went in search of Alex.

He was helping a teenage boy who'd come in while she was in the locker room. She stood a ways off and waited until he was free.

"Sorry. I was busy."

"Of course. Do you have some time to talk to me now? Or should I come by another time?"

"This is the best time."

"Thank you. I wanted to know if any of your women patrons are breast cancer survivors."

By his expression, her question was the last thing he'd expected to hear. "As far as I know, there is only one. She usually comes in at six in the evening."

"If I gave you my cellphone number, would you see that she gets it and ask her to call me?"

"Certainly."

They walked over to the counter and she wrote her name and phone number on the pad he provided.

"Tell her I'm a cancer survivor too, and would like to talk to her."

Alex's eyes softened. "I'll do that."

"Thank you. Could you do me one more favor?"

"Naturally."

"While you are working with your clientele, if you find out any other women are breast cancer survivors too, will you tell them to call me?"

"I'll make a point of finding out."

"I'd appreciate it. I'm in the beginning stages of planning a fun run marathon for us here in Athens. I hope it can be put together by November."

He scratched his head. "I have friends who also manage gyms in the city. I'll pass the word."

"Terrific. See you tomorrow. Same time."

"See you tomorrow, Mrs. Stamatakis."

"Call me Dominique, please."

He grinned. "I was hoping you'd say that."

Her spirits lifted, Dominique left the gym for the hospital. After she'd eaten lunch in the cafeteria, she visited her first patient.

It was like *déjà vu*. Dominique could hear her own fears as she listened to the forty-year-old woman who was about to lose a breast. She asked Dominique the very same questions that had plagued her.

Though the other woman only spoke a little English, they managed to communicate beautifully. Dominique promised she would come in to see her again soon, then made the rounds of several rooms to talk to cancer patients who'd just been checked in.

It was later than she realized when she walked in the penthouse and discovered that Andreas had arrived ahead of her. He had dinner waiting. Over their meal they talked about his newest business venture. She told him about the patients she'd met. Since she had homework, he offered to do the dishes.

The one thing they didn't discuss was Olympia.

It was incredible to her how harmonious everything could be on the surface when they were both aware of a volcano building, ready to erupt.

At ten she closed her textbook, and went to bed first. When Andreas slid under the covers moments later, he reached for her and pulled her back against his chest. "All I want to do is hold you for the rest of the night. Do you mind?"

"Of course not." After a little pause, "Andreas—"

"No more talking. You gave me a lot to think about

last night. Right now I just want to fall asleep with you in my arms. Is that too much to ask?''

''No.''

Nothing was too much to ask. She'd been afraid she'd alienated him to the point he would opt to sleep in the guest bedroom. Unutterably relieved to feel his strong arms wrapped around her, she closed her eyes—only to hear her cellphone ring.

It could be her parents, but she hoped it was the woman from the gym.

''Do you want to get it?'' he asked in his deep voice.

''I think I'd better.''

She sat up against the headboard. He reached for the phone on the bedstand and handed it to her.

''Hello?'' she said, after clicking on.

''This is Dominique?'' a female voice asked in heavily accented English.

''Yes.''

''I am Elektra. Alex said you wanted to talk to me.''

''Yes. Thank you for calling me, Elektra.''

''That is fine. You have cancer too?''

''I did have. I hope it's gone for good.''

''I hope the same thing for me.''

''Do you run as part of your exercise?''

''No, but I think about doing it.''

''Would you mind if I come by the gym tomorrow evening and talk to you after you're finished with your workout?''

''Fine. Seven o'clock. I will look for you.''

''Thank you so much. Goodnight.''

''Goodnight.''

Andreas relieved her of the phone and put it back

on the table. "You've been busy today. Already making inroads on your plans. You're a very remarkable woman, Dominique. I'll go with you tomorrow night and put in a workout."

Her husband was true to his word.

The next evening they both worked out and got acquainted with Elektra. Alex joined in their conversation and said he would help to organize the run. He'd already collected a list of six names for her.

When they reached the penthouse, Dominique made an omelet for them before they went to bed. Andreas didn't try to make love to her. They simply held each other until they fell asleep. It formed a pattern for the rest of the week.

On Friday evening they had dinner at his parents' home. Just the four of them. While Andreas and Eli chatted in the living room, Dominique helped his mother in the kitchen. She'd made her son's favorite dishes.

Before the night was over Dominique had written down the recipes so she could experiment at the penthouse. Everything seemed to be going along so pleasantly, by Saturday she'd almost forgotten their haunting problem.

After breakfast they flew to Zakynthos for a day of swimming and sun. The weather was idyllic. While they lay on mattresses and floated around in the pool, she practiced the Greek she'd learned on Andreas.

He was actually a much better teacher than her tutor at the university. She couldn't imagine ever speaking Greek like a native, but she was determined to try. Andreas was very complimentary.

In truth he was wonderful to her, and waited on her

hand and foot. She felt like a royal princess. Food and drinks appeared before she asked. He turned on music, some soft Greek rock that was so much fun to listen to. Everything from CDs to television helped her pick up the language.

They ended up playing a game where she couldn't say anything unless it was in Greek. At first Andreas asked her easy questions that only required one word answers. Then little by little the answers became more complicated and she started using infinitives instead of conjugated verbs.

He laughed so hard he fell into the pool and pulled her after him. While they were under the water, he kissed her. The kind of kiss he hadn't given her for several days.

When they surfaced, he carried her out of the pool into the house. Eleni caught up with them before they reached the bedroom.

"I'm very sorry to interrupt you, *kyrie*, but Olympia is calling from Athens. She's worried about little Ari and wants to talk to you."

Dominique's guess that Olympia would call about Ari had been close to prophetic. The only thing she'd erred with was that the call had come in the daytime instead of the middle of the night. Still, it worried her to think anything might be seriously wrong with the baby.

"Thank you, Eleni. I'll pick up in our bedroom."

Once they reached it, Andreas lowered Dominique to the floor, then walked over to the bedside table to get the phone.

Most of his conversations with Olympia were brief.

But, like clockwork, he responded by saying he'd be right there.

Over the distance separating them, he shot Dominique an oblique glance.

Oh, my darling Andreas. How you give yourself away.

"Ari's sick and can't stop throwing up. Olympia called the doctor. He told her to take him to the hospital. She's frantic."

She's more than that, only you can't see it.

"Then you have to go."

"Dominique?"

"It's all right. If he's very sick, then she needs your support. But, as you know, I'm the last person she wants to see, so I'll stay here."

Beg me to come with you, Andreas.

He walked toward her. "You're sure?"

Wrong answer, my darling.

"I'm positive."

"I'll try to get back before dark."

You can try, but you won't succeed—because Olympia will find a way to keep you tied to her.

In a lightning move Andreas lowered his head and kissed her with almost suffocating intensity. Once upon a time his display of passion would have been enough to hold her until he came back to make love to her all over again.

But something had snapped inside Dominique since the housekeeper had told them who was on the phone. The more Andreas molded her body to his with barely suppressed savagery, the more she felt distanced from him.

In fact she had the strangest sensation that she was

standing outside her body, aware of what was going on, but no longer with the capacity to derive or give pleasure.

In pure revelation it came to Dominique that Ari was his mother's trump card, one she would play over and over again in the future. There would always be another crisis, another problem, or she would manufacture one.

Theo hadn't given up on his son out of a lack of human feeling. He'd given up because the power of the tie between Olympia and Andreas was too great to contest, let alone break. You could try, but in the end you'd only dash your heart to pieces against it.

Dominique had come back to Greece to fight for her marriage, but she'd arrived at least twenty years too late.

No matter what time Andreas returned to Zakynthos, he wouldn't find her waiting for him. Never again.

It was after ten p.m. when the doctor came into the waiting room of the pediatric ward looking for Olympia. Andreas stood up when he saw him.

"Your baby's going to be fine, Mrs. Panos. You can take him home. He had a bout of gastroenteritis, but the worst has passed. Check with my office tomorrow if you have any more questions."

"Thank you."

In a few minutes they'd bundled little Ari up in the carrycot and left the hospital for Olympia's apartment. Once they were inside and she'd put him to bed, she turned pleading brown eyes to Andreas. "Would you stay with me tonight?"

His mind replayed his wife's warning.

All she has to do is ask, and you come running. It's because for years and years you've been programmed to respond that way, and she knows it. Only she's not a teenager anymore. Her ploys are growing more desperate...

"Where's your aunt?"

"She's gone to my cousin's for the weekend."

More of his conversation with Dominique came back to haunt him.

Her aunt has a nephew? That's news to me. Where does he live?

In Athens.

Then it's very interesting that Olympia would call you to help her with her aunt when there's a nephew nearby.

He's rarely available.

How do you know? Have you talked to him?

Andreas cocked his head. "I thought she was too sick to go anywhere."

"The medicine the doctor gave her made her feel a lot better. I think she wanted to get away from the baby's crying."

No matter what, Olympia always responded with a comment that sounded logical. He'd never bothered to question her. Apparently both he and Maris had been far too naïve when it came to Olympia.

"I'll stay for a while."

"Good. Let me fix us some coffee."

He followed her into the kitchen. In a minute they were sitting across from each other, sipping the steaming hot brew. She looked too happy.

It sickened him to realize how many years he'd been

blind to her machinations. His inability to see through her had brought him dangerously close to losing Dominique.

"Olympia?"

"Would you like a sandwich with that?"

"No, thank you." The time had come. "This can't go on any longer."

"What do you mean?"

He took another swallow, then set his coffee down. "I'm talking about the fantasy world you've been living in since you first became friends with Maris at school."

"Fantasy world?"

"Yes, the one where I'm your husband and Ari is our baby. That's fiction, Olympia. Something you thought up in your head that has no basis in reality. You were a friend of my younger sister. That's all. Because Maris had no guile she couldn't see it in you. Neither could my parents, who included you like you were their own daughter. And Maris was killed before you could be exposed for repaying her loving friendship with a lifetime of insidious treachery."

"Treachery?" she challenged.

"It's as good a word as any to describe your behavior. You've hurt a lot of people, done a lot of damage. Some of it can't be undone, but thank God that doesn't include Dominique."

Her eyes flashed angrily. "She's turned you against me!"

"If you mean she's helped me see into your disturbed psyche, then, yes. I give her full credit. I love my wife with every fiber of my being. She's my priority for the rest of our lives. There's no room for anyone else. Not ever.

"Do you understand what I'm saying?"

Olympia suddenly threw the rest of her coffee in his face. He sat there and let it drip off him.

"By that answer, I see that you do."

Her face crumpled like a child's. Those big brown eyes filled with tears. So many times throughout their lives he'd seen that look and it had brought out his protective instincts.

Andreas was aghast to think how long she'd managed to manipulate him and he'd never caught on.

"How come you never loved me?"

Her question was pathetic, sad, awful.

"How does anyone explain chemistry? It's either there or it isn't. The moment I met Dominique I fell in love with her. Madly, wildly, passionately in love. She transformed my life. That was it for me. She was the one."

"She's not worthy of you!"

"No one asked for your opinion. The fact that you refuse to accept her presence in my life has led you to the point where I've been forced to have this ugly confrontation with you."

"Dominique's not your type."

"She's my exact type!" he countered. "Within seconds my soul, my whole psyche, knew it."

"No!" she cried out in anguish.

"Listen to yourself, Olympia. You're a thirty-year-old woman with a baby. Yet you're carrying on like a spoiled little girl having a temper tantrum. You need help—the kind I certainly can't give you. I'm putting you on notice now. I won't be available to you anymore. The relationship is over. Please don't call or come near me or Dominique again.''

"You don't really mean that—"

"Try me and I'll instruct my attorney to have legal action taken against you. It's the last thing I want to do, but you're out of control.''

She shook her head in denial.

"My wife went to a psychiatrist after she left me. She got therapy to understand herself better. You have eyes and you can see what's happened to her. She's blossomed into the woman who was always there, but was insecure. You could benefit from therapy, Olympia. You're a lovely-looking woman who has insecurities too. Theo left you with enough money to pay for some professional counseling. If I were you I'd seek it, starting tomorrow. Not only for yourself, but for the son you're raising.''

"You talk as if I'm mentally ill.''

"There's something wrong with a woman who claims to have been raped.''

Her features froze.

"I have proof it never happened, Olympia.''

"How do you dare say that to me?''

"This week my attorney went to a judge, who subpoenaed your hospital records. You were never admitted to the emergency room at Acropolis Hospital to be examined, as you claimed. There was no such record because you made up the whole story.''

"I didn't go to that hospital. I went to a private clinic to keep things secret.''

"You know that's not true. Your lies just keep compounding. I found that out when I phoned Theo.''

"He hates you. He would never talk to you.''

"You're wrong. We were friends before you two met. I had a long talk with him about you. I learned firsthand about the hell you put him through. He never physically or emotionally abused you. It was the opposite in fact. For nine months you tormented him by telling him Ari was my baby. You were the one who drove him to charge us with adultery. There's something wrong with a wife who lies to her husband about the paternity of the child he has every right to believe is his."

"He got his wish."

"Only after you extinguished any love he might have had for you. Something else I find unconscionable is the way you destroyed any hope of Paul and Maris getting together. He told me that clear back in high school you made certain the two of them never got together. All because you were sick with jealousy and frustration."

Her teeth clenched. "I hated Paul for always hanging around you. He knew how I felt about you. I could tell he tried to keep us apart."

"As I told you earlier, the chemistry wasn't there, Olympia. Paul didn't have anything to do with it, yet you hurt two people I loved very much. You knew Maris was crazy about him. How cruel was it to feed her lies, making her think Paul didn't care for her?"

"He wasn't good enough for her."

"You can't play with people's lives like that and hope to get away with it forever. When you started to tangle with Dominique, you really got yourself into trouble. I'd say there's a lot wrong with you for purposely and vindictively trying to undermine her confidence. How would you have liked to be twenty-two years old when you heard a diagnosis like hers? How would you have liked being told you needed a mastectomy immediately or you would die?

"Have you ever tried to imagine how she feels when she wakes up every day, wondering if her cancer has come back? Every month she has to take a test, never knowing if it'll turn up positive. Her bravery is something you don't know anything about."

He got to his feet and reached for a nearby towel to wipe himself off. "With professional help you might just be able to approach Theo again and start trying to work things out. No matter what you say, there was a spark there, or Ari wouldn't have been born. He's a wonderful boy. Straighten yourself out before it's too late. You think you're in pain now, but if Ari grows up estranged from you you'll never recover from the pain."

Andreas turned to leave.

"No—please—I love you. You can't go!" She threw herself at him and clung to him. "What will Ari do without you? You're the only man he knows and loves."

"Children are resilient. He'll grow to love someone else. But if you truly love your son you'll do the right thing and get help, so he can at least be united with Theo."

Andreas had to use force to physically remove her before he could leave her apartment. The second he pulled the door closed he heard something crash against it, then came her sobs.

He headed for the limo waiting out in front of the apartment. His pilot was standing by at the airport.

Andreas couldn't get back to Zakynthos and his wife fast enough.

It was after midnight when he raced through the villa to their bedroom. She wasn't there.

"Dominique?"

When there was no answer, he ran out to the pool. "Dominique?"

There was no sign of her. At the thought of her leaving him again, he broke out in a cold sweat.

"Dominique!"

"Kyrie Stamatakis?" He jerked around to discover Eleni, running toward him in her bathrobe. "After lunch she took the estate car and said she was going for a drive. I haven't seen her since."

His heart almost failed him.

With eighty plus miles of coastline, she could be anywhere. She might even have decided to take a commercial chopper back to Athens. He knew she hadn't called his own pilot or he would have been told.

He pulled out his cellphone and called hers. It rang and rang. He left a message, begging her to call him back immediately.

"I'm going to look for her in my car. If by any chance she should call the house or come home, tell her to stay put!"

"I will."

As he drove out onto the main road from the estate, he made a decision to cross over to the eastern side of the island. She'd probably gone to one of the small resort towns along the coast and decided to spend the night at a local hotel.

He passed through Alikanas and Tsilivi, looking for signs of the car in front of every tourist accommodation. When nothing turned up he assumed she'd driven all the way to the town of Zakynthos.

It was a large, bustling place that didn't have the charm it had once had before an earthquake destroyed part of it. But it would be a good place to shop, if that had been her plan.

Or to take a public chopper back to Athens.

After learning from the man in charge of the heliport that she hadn't been a passenger, he breathed more easily and began searching the parking areas of the most reputable hotels—with no success.

After a while he realized it was a lost cause. The only thing to do was make a full circle of the island and then go back to the villa and wait for her to call, or for her to show up in the morning.

Andreas groaned, because it was an exceptionally beautiful night. He ached for his wife. Tonight he had vital news for her.

As the car ate up the miles, he marveled at the full moon bathing the water in light. He was reminded of nights years ago, when he and Paul used to hang out at Laganas, the next town coming up on his left.

Its beach was one of the world's main nesting grounds for endangered Loggerhead sea turtles. The sight brought thousands of tourists to the island, though he, like other environmentalists, hated the influx.

At certain times of the year the turtles climbed onto the beach at night to lay their eggs a foot deep in the sand. Later, when they hatched, the fledglings needed to find their way to the water. The moon lit up the waves to help direct them toward it.

Unfortunately, in the past, lights from cafés and discos had confused the turtles, and many had died of dehydration after moving in the direction of the town.

Andreas had used his influence to help protect the turtles by establishing strict rules to prevent civilization from encroaching on their territory. As a result there was a no-lights curfew, no umbrellas permitted in the sand, no digging, no dogs, no boats, and no talking to disturb nature's precious system for preserving the species.

The tourists who flocked here at this time of year to see the babies hatching were now forced to observe the fascinating phenomenon from the place where the wild grass met the sand. Thus the fledglings wouldn't be startled or tormented, unless it was by seabirds on the hunt for food.

He'd always intended to bring Dominique here. But she'd left Greece before that could happen, plunging him into a black void of despair. "At the next full moon," he'd promised her.

As the words left his lips, he felt the hairs prickle on the back of his neck. Something told him he might find her here.

She *had* to be here. He couldn't think beyond that.

At the bend in the road he slowed down and cruised by the designated parking area. Relief washed over him when he discovered the estate car among the others. He pulled into the first free place and got out.

After walking a few yards he spotted her, lying at the edge of the grass on her stomach. She'd separated herself from everyone else.

He hadn't needed to worry that it would take him time to spot her, not with her glorious silvery-gold mane illuminated by the moonlight. Talk about heavenly foxfire.

CHAPTER TEN

DOMINIQUE did what the other tourists were doing and lay on her stomach. Signs had been posted everywhere, warning the tourists to stay invisible. She tried not to move while she waited to see signs of turtle activity along the beach.

If she hadn't heard some people talking about the full moon tonight she would have been on the next plane to Kefalonia. From there she would have taken another plane to Athens, before booking through to Sarajevo as her final destination.

But this was a sight she'd always wanted to see. What was another six hours before she left Greece? With Ari in the hospital, it might be another day before Andreas felt he could leave.

For now she pushed that pain to the nethermost region of her heart and concentrated on a phenomenon of nature that could only be viewed here and at a few other rare spots on earth.

She'd been lying there several hours, anticipating the moment when she would see movement. Maybe there wouldn't be any. Some of the tourists had already given up their vigil.

A few more minutes and she detected footfall behind her. She looked around. Her body quickened when she discovered who was staring down at her.

Andreas put a finger to his lips to stop her from making any noise. In the next instant he'd stretched himself out next to her and slid his arm around her shoulders.

For the moment they had to refrain from communicating with words. It was just as well. She couldn't deal with any more pain right now. Besides, his nearness had caused her heart to thud so hard and fast she was afraid the baby turtles would sense the vibration through the tons of sand.

While she kept her eyes trained on the beach, she could feel Andreas's gaze studying her profile. She didn't dare look at him. Her emotions were in far too much turmoil.

Another ten minutes passed. Suddenly he applied a little pressure to her shoulder, alerting her that he'd noticed something. He was staring across the sand to the left.

She followed his gaze. Sure enough, about ten feet off, she saw two little turtles no bigger than fifty cent pieces surface and start making their way toward the foam.

It was a magical moment.

Her eyes filled with tears. She held her breath, hoping they would make it to the water without incident. The danger from predators was great, and a large percentage of them perished.

Andreas had once told her that scientists believed the magnetic field of the earth got imprinted in their brains during their struggle across the beach. That imprint enabled them to find their way back here in twenty years to lay their own eggs.

She found the whole experience indescribably moving.

At the end of an hour, the little babies had reached the water. Other fish and crabs were probably waiting for them now they'd disappeared in the ocean, but she was so relieved they'd made it that far she wanted to cry for joy.

Unable to help herself, she turned her head to look at her husband. She discovered moist black eyes fastened on her.

No matter what the future held, she was thankful he'd found her in time to witness something that had become a spiritual experience for both of them.

In one lithe movement, he got to his feet and pulled her up with him. Without a sound passing between them, they quietly made their way back to the parking area.

After helping her into the estate car he whispered in his deep male voice, ''Follow me.''

She waited until he'd driven out to the road, then stayed right behind him. He drove another two minutes before entering a marina, where there was a speedboat rental shop. She pulled in next to him and got out of the car.

Though it was the middle of the night, her husband showed no hesitation in knocking at the door of the cabin next to the office to waken the owner.

The older man who answered in a bathrobe greeted Andreas with a clap on the shoulder and a hearty welcome. They spoke in Greek. While she waited outside, they went into his office.

In a few minutes the owner came out with a set of keys. Andreas trailed, carrying a cooler. He'd obviously planned an outing for them. Her reward for being a good wife while he'd been gone to help Olympia with her son?

Pain pierced her heart, robbing her of the joy he wanted to give her. Not willing to make a scene, she walked behind them and climbed in the boat. Andreas placed the cooler on the floor before handing her a life jacket to put on.

The proprietor untied the ropes, giving Andreas the signal to start the motor. They reversed before heading out into the bay. The owner waved them off with a smile, unaware of Dominique's turmoil.

To him it probably looked romantic. A couple out for a moonlight picnic.

Her husband flashed her a covert glance. "The ocean's calm tonight. Lie back against the seat and enjoy the view."

His nearness created havoc with her senses. "Are we going far?"

"Let me surprise you."

She had to admit the next hour was one of enchantment. They followed the coastline up the northwest side of the island. The panorama changed from lush fertile land to towering cliffs. He brought the boat in close, to see them at their greatest advantage. They were so steep she got dizzy when she looked all the way up their sheer walls.

Here and there she glimpsed secret coves and impossibly white beaches that appeared untouched by humans. The powerfully built man at the helm, with his disheveled black hair and penetrating eyes, might well be a descendant of the ancient Achaean pirates, stealing her away to a lonely grotto only he knew about.

Something in his demeanor sent a delicious shiver through her body. He was the same man she'd married, yet he wasn't. Few words had passed between them, making her the slightest bit nervous in an exciting, breathless kind of way.

She'd thought she knew everything about her husband, but the possessiveness in the curl of his hard mouth added a new dimension that made the blood sing in her veins.

The boat cleaved through the water faster and faster. He had a definite destination in mind. A few more minutes and she let out a gasp to see Shipwreck Beach before them. Andreas's backyard.

The pristine beach was hemmed in on three sides by tall, gigantic cliffs. It was a difficult place to reach. You could take a footpath after parking your car way back on the road. But the best way to visit it was by water.

She'd been down here with him once before, but only during the day, when boatloads of tourists stopped for a brief look on their tour of the island. An old rusted hull of a ship, stranded in a storm years earlier, lay in the middle of the sand.

Tonight they had the whole place to themselves beneath a full moon that made the oceanscape surreal. Not a soul was in sight. They could be the last two people on earth.

She saw fire glint in the black depths of his eyes. He wanted to make love to her here in this paradise he'd loved from boyhood. She sensed his excitement at being here alone with her, away from the world.

The palpable sensual tension had been building between them since they'd lain together on the grass watching the turtles.

Dominique was furious with herself for feeling this weakness around him. Earlier tonight she'd been on the verge of leaving for Sarajevo. Yet here she was, full of desire for her husband.

If she gave in to her longings now, it meant something was wrong with her. It would be clear to Andreas that she was willing to put up with Olympia in their lives because she couldn't give him up.

"No, don't—" she cried when he cut the engine.

Shadows darkened his features. "What do you mean, don't?"

"I—I want to go back to our cars."

"It's too late," he said in a grating voice.

In front of her astonished gaze he walked to the back of the boat and jumped into the water in order to push them up on the sand. Before she could blink, he swam around to her side and lifted her bodily from the boat, with her life jacket still on.

He was big and moved like an athlete. Carrying her in a fireman's hold, he walked up the beach with her as if she weighed no more than a couple of cotton balls.

"Wait here." His lips grazed hers before he went back to the boat for the cooler. When he returned a second time, with blankets he'd no doubt pulled from one of the lockers beneath the padded bench, her fingers still covered lips that hadn't stopped tingling from the electrifying contact.

He spread out one blanket on the sand. When he removed his shirt, he looked like a statue of a Greek god come to life. In the moonlight she felt bewitched by him.

Frightened of his power over her, she averted her eyes. "I can't do this."

"Can't do what? Love me like you did when you came back to try and make our marriage work?"

"I—I made that request before I realized some marriages aren't fixable."

"I agree with that statement—if the husband and wife aren't both fighting for it with every breath in their bodies."

"Sometimes not even that is enough."

He closed the distance between them and removed her life jacket. "Look at me."

She shook her head. "It's no use, Andreas."

As she struggled to pull away he said, "Tonight I made certain Olympia is out of our lives forever."

"I'd like to believe that." Her voice trembled. "But we bo—"

"Did you hear me?" he demanded, shaking her gently but firmly. "I threatened her with a protective order. She understands that if she ever tries to come near I'll have her prosecuted."

Dominique's head reared back. To her chagrin, hot tears trickled down her cheeks. "That won't stop her. She knows how to get to you."

"I was afraid you wouldn't believe me, and I understand why. So I brought you proof."

He reached in his trouser pocket and pulled out a mini tape recorder. "What you're going to hear is the conversation we had after we took Ari home and put him to bed. Just so you know, he's got gastroenteritis, but he's going to be fine."

Dominique was glad to hear the good news, but she was still reeling from the sight of the recorder in his hand. "You taped it?"

"Yes. Let's lie down and we'll both listen. If you're wondering why I've removed my shirt, there are several reasons. One of them being that at a certain point in our conversation she threw her coffee at me in a violent rage."

He lay down on his side and patted the space next to him. In a daze, Dominique knelt in front of him and reached for his shirt. Huge stains had ruined the elegant cream silk material.

She let out a low moan and ran her fingers over his face and jaw. "Did she burn you?"

He caught her hand and kissed it. "No. By the time she lost control it had cooled."

"Andreas—"

She watched him press the button on the recorder. Out of the stillness of the night came their voices.

Would you stay with me tonight?

Where's your aunt?

She's gone to my cousin's for the weekend.

I thought she was too sick to go anywhere.

The medicine the doctor gave her made her feel a lot better. I think she wanted to get away from the baby's crying.

I'll stay for a while.

Good. Let me fix us some coffee.

Olympia?

Would you like a sandwich with that?

No, thank you. This can't go on any longer.

What do you mean?

I'm talking about the fantasy world you've been living in since you first became friends with Maris at school.

Fantasy world?

Yes, the one where I'm your husband and Ari is our baby. That's fiction, Olympia. Something you thought up in your head that has no basis in reality. You were a friend of my younger sister. That's all. Because Maris had no guile, she couldn't see it in you. Neither could my parents, who included you like you were their own daughter. And Maris was killed before you could be exposed for repaying her loving friendship with a lifetime of insidious treachery.

Treachery?

It's as good a word as any to describe your behavior. You've hurt a lot of people, done a lot of damage. Some of it can't be undone, but thank God that doesn't include Dominique.

She's turned you against me!

If you mean she's helped me see into your disturbed psyche, then, yes. I give her full credit.

With every revelation Dominique felt a lifting of the terrible crushing pain that had plagued their marriage for so long. When the tape came to an end, she'd drenched herself and him in tears.

"It's over," she whispered. "Really over."

He stared deeply into her eyes. "Let tonight be the real beginning of our marriage."

Her heart was too full to talk.

His beautiful smile swept her away.

"We're two shipwrecked lovers washed up on a distant shore for life. We have the moon to give us light, the sand to give us warmth. Best of all we have our bodies to give each other joy. Come here to me, my love."

Dominique hugged both her parents at the same time. "I'm so glad you're here to see the fun run. After this is over we'll fly to Zakynthos with Eli and Bernice and fix our own Thanksgiving feast. It'll be a first for them."

"After this run, you're going to need to relax. Your father and I will do the cooking."

"Andreas will thank you."

I'll thank you. For the last week Dominique hadn't been very hungry. She'd attributed it to nerves, because she wanted this first marathon to go without a hitch.

"I'm so proud of you for organizing all this I could burst."

"Thanks, Dad. A hundred runners aren't bad for the first one."

"It's fantastic," her mother murmured. "Darling? I think they're about ready to start. Good luck. After we can't see you anymore we're going to drive to the finish line to join Andreas and his parents. They're already there with the camera, waiting for you."

She felt her dad's probing eyes. "You okay, Domani?"

"I've never been better."

"Sure?"

"Maybe I've got a little stage fright. I don't want to do anything to embarrass Andreas."

"Embarrass—" her parents cried at the same time.

"You know. Stumble and fall flat on my face. I'd die if I did that."

Her dad frowned. "You've never done it before. Do you feel a little shaky or something?"

"No. I guess I'd better go. See you soon."

She kissed both their cheeks before dashing off to join the others.

Alex from the gym was one of the volunteers helping coordinate the drive-along cars and first-aid people. What a wonderful man and friend he'd turned out to be!

He helped her put on her number. "May you come in first, Dominique!"

"May I come in, period!"

His laughter trailed her as she joined the pack and waited for the gun to go off. Her throat almost closed with emotion to see all these women who'd fought the odds and won. So much power was in this group. Such faith and determination.

Her eyes met Elektra's. They were moist too.

This was a special sisterhood. Everyone could feel it.

Pop!

Dominique took off at a moderate pace beneath an overcast sky. The cooler temperature made it perfect for running. She didn't care if she came in last. Her one priority was to finish a good race.

Quite a crowd had assembled along the route. One of the local stations was televising it. Her husband's name had opened doors that would have been closed to her efforts otherwise.

How she loved him.

No man in the world could equal him. He'd seen her at her worst and loved her. Today she wanted him to see her at her best. She wanted him to be proud of her.

The 15k race had markers every so often, to let the runners know their progress. Dominique stayed near the back of the pack, unwilling to push herself.

At the halfway point she noticed several of the women had started walking. The crowd clapped and cheered for them. That thrilled Dominique, because it meant these people recognized this was all in aid of cancer awareness.

If just one woman in the crowd decided to get herself checked in time to stop the disease, then this run would have been worth it.

At the three-quarter mark Dominique suddenly felt nauseated. Her body broke out in a cold sweat. There was a ringing in her ears before her legs gave away.

When she became cognizant again, she discovered she was in an ambulance with an IV in her arm.

She looked at the two paramedics. "What happened to me?"

One of them was checking her pulse. "You fainted."

"I can't believe I did that."

He smiled. "It happened to several runners today."

"I've never fainted in my life."

"Have you had a cold? Fever?" the other one asked. "No. Nothing."

"They'll get you checked out at the hospital."

"Oh, no—" she groaned. "My husband's waiting for me at the finish line! He'll be frantic when I don't show up. He has a cellphone. Will someone call him?"

"What's his name?"

"Andreas Stamatakis."

The name galvanized the man into action. "Give me his number."

In a minute he said, "Your husband's not answering. I wouldn't be surprised if he's at the hospital waiting for you."

The paramedic's words were prophetic. As they put her on a gurney and started to roll her inside Andreas rushed out to her, his face white.

He bent down and kissed her lips. "Thank God you're awake."

"I only fainted."

"Alex relayed the message. Our parents are on their way. Come on. Let's get you inside."

Within the next few minutes an emergency room

physician came into the cubicle to examine her. He asked Andreas to step outside. She could tell he didn't like it at all, but he had to comply.

"That's an anxious husband you've got there." He smiled. "I've seen the paramedics' report. Your vitals are fine. You seem recovered. So I'm going to ask you a question, because it might save us a lot of trouble. Could you be pregnant?"

She blinked. Could she? "We've been trying for a couple of months."

"Well, then. We'll do a test right now. If it's positive, that would explain your fainting spell."

"Wait—"

"Yes?"

"Don't let on to my husband yet. If we're expecting a baby, I want to tell him myself."

He winked. "Understood. I'll tell him to go to the reception area and wait. In the meantime we'll get your blood work started, and I'll send in a nurse for the test."

"I hope I'm pregnant," she said when the nurse came in.

"We'll know in a few minutes."

By the time her blood had been drawn, the nurse had returned. She handed the test device to Dominique. "Take a look."

"There's a red line! I can't believe it!"

"Do you want me to send your husband back in?"

"Oh, yes! Please!"

Before long Andreas had rushed inside the cubicle. The fear in his eyes was too much. All she wanted to do was take it away.

"I hope you're ready to be a father, because we're going to have a baby."

He didn't say anything. He didn't have to.

His face underwent a total transformation. Before she knew it he was bent over her, sobbing quietly into her neck.

She caressed the back of his dark, handsome head. "I know you thought my collapse meant something terrible was wrong with me."

"I couldn't bear to lose you, Dominique."

"No one's going to lose anyone. Isn't it incredible that an accident during my first race in Greece brought you into my life? And now a fainting spell during my second race means we're getting a son or daughter to raise. I'm thinking Maris if it's a girl, and Paul if it's a boy. Why don't you go tell our parents and see if they approve?"

His hands clutched her tighter. "I don't want to leave you."

"One minute is all it will take. Think what it will mean to them."

He raised up and wiped his gorgeous black eyes. "Half a minute."

"Go on."

Andreas pressed his mouth to hers, then slipped behind the curtain.

She didn't have to wait long to hear cries of joy and the sound of footsteps rushing toward her.

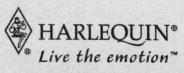

If you enjoyed what you just read,
then we've got an offer you can't resist!

Take 2 bestselling
love stories FREE!
Plus get a FREE surprise gift!

Clip this page and mail it to Harlequin Reader Service®

IN U.S.A.	**IN CANADA**
3010 Walden Ave.	P.O. Box 609
P.O. Box 1867	Fort Erie, Ontario
Buffalo, N.Y. 14240-1867	L2A 5X3

YES! Please send me 2 free Harlequin Romance® novels and my free surprise gift. After receiving them, if I don't wish to receive anymore, I can return the shipping statement marked cancel. If I don't cancel, I will receive 6 brand-new novels every month, before they're available in stores! In the U.S.A., bill me at the bargain price of $3.57 plus 25¢ shipping & handling per book and applicable sales tax, if any*. In Canada, bill me at the bargain price of $4.05 plus 25¢ shipping & handling per book and applicable taxes**. That's the complete price and a savings of 10% off the cover prices—what a great deal! I understand that accepting the 2 free books and gift places me under no obligation ever to buy any books. I can always return a shipment and cancel at any time. Even if I never buy another book from Harlequin, the 2 free books and gift are mine to keep forever.

186 HDN DZ72
386 HDN DZ73

Name	(PLEASE PRINT)

Address	Apt.#

City	State/Prov.	Zip/Postal Code

Not valid to current Harlequin Romance® subscribers.
Want to try another series? Call 1-800-873-8635
or visit www.morefreebooks.com.

* Terms and prices subject to change without notice. Sales tax applicable in N.Y.
** Canadian residents will be charged applicable provincial taxes and GST.
   All orders subject to approval. Offer limited to one per household.
   ® are registered trademarks owned and used by the trademark owner and or its licensee.

HROM04R   ©2004 Harlequin Enterprises Limited

SLEUTHING, SUSPENSE AND SIZZLING ROMANCE.

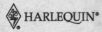 HARLEQUIN®

INTRIGUE®

HAS IT ALL.

Each month we bring you the best in breathtaking romantic suspense that will keep you on the edge of your seat.

DON'T MISS A SINGLE BOOK!

Available at your favorite retail outlet.

www.eHarlequin.com

HIGEN05